The Case of the Tenacious Tibetan

A Thousand Islands Doggy Inn Mystery

B.R. Snow

Website: www.brsnow.net/

Twitter: @BernSnow

Facebook: facebook.com/bernsnow

Cover Design: Reggie Cullen

Cover Photo: James R. Miller

Other Books by B.R. Snow

The Thousand Islands Doggy Inn Mysteries

- The Case of the Abandoned Aussie
- The Case of the Brokenhearted Bulldog
- The Case of the Caged Cockers
- The Case of the Dapper Dandie Dinmont
- The Case of the Eccentric Elkhound
- The Case of the Faithful Frenchie
- The Case of the Graceful Goldens
- The Case of the Hurricane Hounds
- The Case of the Itinerant Ibizan
- The Case of the Jaded Jack Russell
- The Case of the Klutz King Charles
- The Case of the Lovable Labs
- The Case of the Mellow Maltese
- The Case of the Natty Newfie
- The Case of the Overdue Otterhound
- The Case of the Prescient Poodle
- The Case of the Quizzical Queens Beagle
- The Case of the Reliable Russian Spaniels
- The Case of the Salubrious Soft Coated Wheaten
- The Case of Italian Indigestion (A Josie and Chef Claire Sojourn)

The Whiskey Run Chronicles

- The Whiskey Run Chronicles – The Complete Volume 1
- The Whiskey Run Chronicles – The Complete Volume 2

The Damaged Posse

- American Midnight
- Larrikin Gene
- Sneaker World
- Summerman
- The Duplicates

Other Books

- Divorce Hotel
- Either Ore

To Connie

and all the Cavallario family

Chapter 1

I scanned the shelves and let my eyes wander left and right, up and down. Undecided, I sighed loudly then heard Chief Abrams clear his throat. I glanced over my shoulder and, despite his attempt to remain patient, I couldn't miss his tight-lipped grimace.

"Sorry, Chief."

"Too many choices?"

"I guess."

"What are you looking for?"

"I'm not sure," I said, rocking back and forth on my heels as I continued to scan the snack food aisle. "Something salty, but still relatively healthy."

"Salty, huh?" he said, joining the search. "The other day you were on a sweet kick."

"At least I'm not predictable," I said, reaching for a can of almonds. "This will do."

"Finally."

"And maybe some cashews," I said, grabbing a second can. "Okay, I'm good to go. You want anything?"

"No, I'll save myself for dinner," Chief Abrams said. "And if we don't get out on the River soon, we'll just drive to the restaurant from here."

"Funny," I said, heading for checkout.

We got in line, and I saw Jackson, the store owner and Clay Bay's former chief of police, working the cash register. A man I didn't know was standing behind Jackson studying his movements. I spotted a rack of sundries near the register and again let my eyes wander left and right, up and down.

"Do I want a candy bar?" I said, more to the rack than the Chief.

"I thought you were craving salty."

"I am," I said, my eyes landing on Reese's peanut butter cups. "Perfect." I grabbed two and smiled at the Chief. "But this one gives me both salty and sweet. I get the best of both worlds."

"So, it's sort of like the candy bar version of surf and turf?"

"Exactly," I said, nodding as we reached the head of the line. "Hey, Jackson. What are you doing working the register?"

"Hi, Suzy," he said, eyeing my selections. "Jodie called in sick, and Tom had to take his mom to the doctor. So, here I am. Hey, Chief."

"Hi, Jackson," Chief Abrams said.

"Day off?" Jackson said.

"I worked this morning," the Chief said, glancing at his watch. "We're heading out to do a little fishing before it gets dark."

"You better hurry," Jackson said, running the items across the scanner. "How are you feeling, Suzy?"

"I'm good." I smiled at the man standing next to Jackson and extended my hand. "I'm Suzy Chandler."

"Nice to meet you," the man said, returning the handshake. "I'm Joshua Williams."

"I'm sorry," Jackson said. "How rude of me. Joshua, this is Chief Abrams, our local chief of police. And Suzy runs the Doggy Inn."

"Nice to meet you," the Chief said, shaking hands.

"Likewise. What's a Doggy Inn?" Joshua said with a frown.

"It's kind of a one-stop shop for all things dog," I said. "Vet services, groom and board, rescue program, stuff like that."

"What a great line of work," Joshua said, smiling.

"Yeah, we like it," I said.

"Joshua is thinking about buying the store," Jackson said.

"Really?" I said, glancing back and forth at both men.

"It's looking good," Joshua said, smiling as he looked around the store. "In fact, if you don't mind, Jackson, I think I'll go take another look at some of those numbers."

"Knock yourself out," Jackson said.

"It was nice meeting you," Joshua said, then headed off with a wave.

We watched him go then I focused on Jackson.

"You finally found a buyer. Congratulations, Jackson."

"Thanks," Jackson said. "And if I never see a case of vegetables again, it won't break my heart."

"Who's the buyer?" Chief Abrams said.

"He's originally from Buffalo," Jackson said. "But he's been living in Texas for several years. Says he misses the seasons and wants to relocate back to a colder climate."

"Well, mission accomplished," I said. "How much do I owe you?"

"$17.50," Jackson said. "He wants a place on the River. I'm including my camp in the deal."

"You're selling your cabin?" the Chief said.

"Yeah," Jackson said with a coy smile. "I'm not gonna need it. I've got my eye on Casper Island."

"You're buying Casper?" I said, surprised.

"Yeah, I don't think I can pass it up," Jackson said. "The Newtons are finally ready to sell. It's just too much for them to handle."

"I get that," I said. "They're both in their eighties, right?"

"They are," Jackson said, accepting the twenty I was holding out. "Fishing, huh? I hope you dressed warm."

"It might be the last chance we'll get before I take the boat out of the water," I said. "Are you coming to Thanksgiving dinner at the restaurant?"

"Of course," Jackson said, putting the items in a plastic bag. "I'll probably be at the last seating. I'm going to be open Thanksgiving morning. You know, just in case some folks forget a few things."

"What a nice thing to do," I said.

"It'll be the last time I do it," Jackson said, beaming. "After that, I begin my new life."

"New horizons, huh?" the Chief said.

"Let me guess," I deadpanned. "Yoga instructor?"

"Funny. Nice to see pregnancy hasn't affected your blinding wit," Jackson said. "Actually, I'm going into business as a fishing guide."

"Good for you," the Chief said. "Getting paid to fish. I wish I'd thought of that."

"Say, we're all meeting for dinner at C's if you'd like to join us," I said.

"I wish I could," Jackson said. "But I'm really short-staffed today. Ask me again in a couple of weeks. Knock on wood."

"Will do," I said, grabbing the bag and turning to the Chief. "Are you ready?"

"You're asking me?"

"Speaking of blinding wit," I said, making a face at him. "Let's go. It's gonna be dark soon. Later, Jackson."

"Have fun."

Chief Abrams and I headed outside toward my SUV.

"He's a happy man," the Chief said.

"He's been thinking about selling for a long time," I said.

"Can't blame him. The hours are brutal."

"Yeah," I said, opening one of the peanut butter cups. "I wouldn't want to do it."

"But think about being surrounded by all that food on a daily basis."

"I'd be constantly restocking. Hey, Rooster."

"Hi, guys," Rooster said as he climbed out of his truck. As usual, he was under-dressed for the weather; a cold, blustery November afternoon. "What's up?"

"We're heading out to do some fishing," I said. "You want to join us?"

"I would, but I need to do some grocery shopping," he said. "The larder is almost bare."

"You coming to dinner tonight?" I said.

"Wouldn't miss it," Rooster said. "Chef Claire said she has another new Italian dish she wants to try out on us."

"Another one?" the Chief said. "Man, she's on a roll since she and Josie got back."

"Yeah, she should travel more often," Rooster said. "But I'd be there just for the new bread you guys are serving. That stuff is addicting. What time should I be there?"

"Around seven is good," I said.

"See you then," Rooster said with a wave as he headed for the store entrance.

"Shorts in late November?" the Chief said, shaking his head. "How the heck does he do it?"

"He's a tough old bird," I said, grinning as I watched Rooster disappear from sight. "Okay, let's go wet a line."

"You need any help getting in the car?"

"A fat joke? Really, Chief?"

"Not at all," he said, heading for the passenger door. "I was merely trying to be a gentleman."

"Sorry," I said. "I guess I'm getting a little sensitive. Hormone imbalance and all that."

"I'll take your word for it."

We made the short drive back to the Inn and headed straight for the dock. The Chief climbed into the boat and waited for me to join him. I looked back and forth at the boat then down at my feet that were planted firmly on the dock.

"Okay, I need some help getting in."

"I know," he said, stifling a laugh.

"But you weren't going to offer, right?"

"Not a chance," he said, extending both hands.

I grabbed them then slowly lowered myself into the boat.

"Crap."

"What's the matter?" the Chief said.

"I should have untied the lines before I got in."

"I'll get them," he said.

"Thanks," I said, starting the engine. "We really are getting a late start. We might want to stay close to home."

"Not a problem," he said, tossing the lines onto the boat. "Let's check out Grovenor shoal."

"We hardly ever catch fish there," I said, backing away from the dock.

"Then you'll be able to snack in peace, right?"

"Works for me," I said, accelerating as I swung the boat around. "Maybe we can get an earlier start tomorrow."

"Tomorrow?" he said. "Yeah, I think I can make it. As long as no major police business pops up."

"I like your chances. It is the quiet time of year."

"Shhh. Don't jinx it."

Chapter 2

I cut through the crisp breading into a layer of mushrooms stacked on top of a marinated chicken breast pounded thin and immediately felt my knife touch the plate. Impressed, as always, by Chef Claire's technique, I knew the dish was delicious even before I tasted it. I slid a forkful into my mouth and savored. I swallowed, put my knife and fork down, and took a sip of fizzy water before glancing around the table.

"I'm glad I'm sitting down," I said to no one in particular.

"It's unbelievable," Josie said. "It cuts like butter."

"How does she do it?" Paulie said, gently squeezing my mother's hand before resuming his attack on the Milanese chicken.

"She has a gift," my mother said, then glanced at Josie. "How many more Italian recipes does she have in store for us?"

"A bunch, I think," Josie said, making short work of her dinner.

"You should go away more often," my mother said, then laughed and glanced around the half-filled restaurant. "Not a bad crowd for November."

"I see a bunch of people who are in town for Thanksgiving," I said. "And some college kids are already home for the holidays."

"Makes sense," my mother said, nodding as she cut another piece of the breaded cutlet. "I remember taking you to dinner when you'd come home on school break. Offering to feed you was the only way I ever got to see you."

"Funny, Mom."

One of the kitchen doors swung open, and Chef Claire emerged dressed in white and wearing her chef hat. She headed straight for our table and sat down next to me.

"Nice hat," Josie deadpanned.

"It's time for some new material," Chef Claire said, making a face at her before pouring herself a glass of wine. She took a sip and nodded her approval. "How's dinner?"

"Unbelievable," I said, patting her hand. "How do you get the chicken so tender?"

"I beat the crap out of it with my bat then marinate it overnight," Chef Claire said, then took another sip of wine.

"Your bat?" Paulie said.

"She's joking," my mother said, then glanced at Chef Claire. "You are joking, right, dear?"

"Yes, Mrs. C.," Chef Claire said, grinning. "I don't use my bat. But I do beat the crap out of it. Normally, I'd make it with turkey, but since we're so close to Thanksgiving, I thought I'd use chicken."

"Good call," Josie said, nodding her approval.

"Where's the Chief?" Chef Claire said. "He told me he was coming tonight."

"He said he had a few things to take care of before dinner," I said.

"Did you guys catch any fish this afternoon?" Chef Claire said.

"Actually, we did," I said. "But we got out there late and ran out of light. You'll never guess what we saw on our way back."

"The sunset," my mother said.

"You're worse than her," I said, nodding at Josie.

"What was it?" Chef Claire said, topping off everyone's glass.

"A bear cub," I said.

"Really?" Paulie said. "Where?"

"It was on Enchantment Island."

"Isn't that where Jackson's camp is?" Paulie said.

"That's the one," I said. "I couldn't believe it. How the heck did a bear cub get on an island?"

"My guess would be it swam," Paulie said. "But Enchantment is pretty isolated. It has to be a couple of miles from anything."

"Yeah, it is," I said. "The Chief was going to put a call into Fish and Wildlife."

"Any sign of momma bear?" Chef Claire said.

"No. The cub was on the dock all by itself."

"Doing what?" Josie said.

"It was just sitting there," I said. "Almost like it was standing guard."

"Well, if its mother is around, I hope the folks from Fish and Wildlife are careful," Paulie said. "Mama bears are incredibly protective of their cubs."

We all looked up when we saw Chief Abrams approaching the table. He gave us a small wave then sat down next to Josie.

"Sorry I'm late," he said, accepting the glass of wine Chef Claire had poured. "I had a heck of a time tracking down the right person from Fish and Wildlife."

"What did they have to say?" I said.

"They're sending somebody out first thing in the morning," the Chief said, glancing around at everyone's plate. "I take it everyone had the special."

"We did," I said. "Highly recommended."

"Now, there's a surprise," he said, raising his glass in salute to Chef Claire.

She returned the salute and finished the last of her wine.

"One chicken-mushroom Milanese coming up," she said, getting to her feet. "It won't take long."

"Thanks, Chef Claire," the Chief said, then sipped his wine.

"Did Fish and Wildlife have any guesses about how the bear cub got there?" I said.

"They assume it swam," Chief Abrams said. "It's the only thing that makes any sense. I doubt if anybody gave it a ride."

"Are we still going fishing in the morning?" I said.

"I'm in if you are. But it's going to be cold, so bundle up," the Chief said.

"Please don't overdo it, darling."

"I'll be fine, Mom. Don't worry, your granddaughter will be snug as a bug in a rug."

"Okay," she said, nodding.

"That's it?"

"What?"

"You gave up without a fight," I said, beaming at her. "I should have gotten pregnant years ago."

"You'll get no argument from me," she said, smiling back. "But please be careful out there."

"You got it, Mom. And I promise not to get within a mile of the bear."

"Good," my mother said, then sat back in her chair and glanced around the table. "Now, there's something I'd like to discuss with all of you."

"Sure," I said, taking a sip of water. "What's on your mind?"

"Cayman."

"What about it?" I said, glancing at Josie.

"I'm not sure you're going to like what I'm about to say."

"What are the odds?" I deadpanned.

"Don't start," my mother said as she fixed a hard stare on me. "I think we should skip our trip to the islands this year."

"Really?" I said.

"Yes, I do," she said, nodding. "Given your condition and the fact your doctor won't be around, I'm not comfortable with the idea. And it's so hot down there. I can't imagine you'd be comfortable."

"You think I'll be more comfortable in minus ten and three feet of snow?"

"Actually, darling, yes, I do. And you can sit in front of the fire in those dreadful sweatpants relaxing all winter."

"They're comfy. It's interesting you say that, Mom."

"How's that?"

"Because we were just talking about the same thing last night."

"We were," Josie said, nodding. "And we like the idea."

"Have the planets suddenly aligned?" my mother said to Paulie.

"I told you she'd listen to reason," Paulie said, nodding as he looked at me. "Are you sure you're okay with the idea?"

"I am," I said. "We haven't done a winter here in a while. It might be fun."

"I think fun might be a bit of a stretch," Josie said. "But Chef Claire is very excited about the idea."

"Chef Claire loves snowmobiling and cross-country skiing," my mother said to Paulie.

"Chef Claire is nuts," Josie said.

"Who's nuts?" Chef Claire said as she approached the table carrying Chief Abram's dinner.

"You are," Josie said. "We were just discussing the prospect of spending winter here."

"I can't wait," Chef Claire said, sitting back down at the table.

"I rest my case," Josie said.

"This is incredible, Chef Claire," the Chief said, digging into his meal.

"Thanks, Chief," she said, glancing around the dining room. "I think the rush is over, so I'm going to have another glass of wine." She poured then focused on my mother. "Will you still be going to Cayman, Mrs. C.?"

"Not a chance," my mother said.

Josie and I both snorted.

"I'll need to get down there at least once," Chef Claire said. "Just to check on the restaurant. But I shouldn't be gone for more than a week."

"Oh, I forgot to tell you," I said, glancing around the table. "The Chief and I were at Jackson's today. It looks like he found a buyer for the store."

"Good for him," my mother said. "Nobody should have to work hours like that. Who's the buyer?"

"Some guy named Joshua Williams," I said. "He's moving back to the area from Texas. He grew up in Buffalo and apparently misses winter."

"He sounds perfect for you," Josie said to Chef Claire.

"Yeah, I'll keep that in mind," Chef Claire said, gently punching Josie on the shoulder.

"Jackson's also selling his camp to him," the Chief said.

"Really?" Paulie said. "He loves that place."

"He's got his eye on Casper Island," I said.

"Nice," Paulie said, nodding. "It's a beautiful island."

"And he's talking about becoming a fishing guide," the Chief said.

"From cop to grocery store owner to fishing guide," my mother said. "Not what I'd call a traditional career path. But if that's what makes him happy, right?"

"Exactly," I said, raising my water glass in a toast. "To Jackson."

"To Jackson," everyone said in unison, then sipped their wine.

"Should he call it an add-on or a feature?" Josie said.

"English, please," I said, frowning at her.

"The bear," she said. "You said you saw it near Jackson's camp. So, I was just wondering how he should describe it to the new owner."

Everyone laughed.

"A part of the authentic native environment?" Chef Claire said.

"Good one," Josie said. "Nature at its finest."

"Or a security system," I said, grinning.

"There you go," Josie said, nodding. "A security system that eats intruders."

Chapter 3

I let the dogs out to take care of business then got them settled down back inside. Before I even finished my coffee, all four were sprawled and snoring contentedly in the living room. A half-hour later, I headed down to the dock armed with a backpack of snacks and a thermos of coffee. I spotted Chief Abram's car pulling into the parking lot and waited as he made the short walk to the boat.

"Good morning," I said, giving him a quick hug. "Perfect timing."

"Good morning," he said, reaching for the backpack. "Let me carry that for you."

"Hey, I forgot to ask you last night. How's the new puppy working out?" I said as we strolled down the dock.

"She's a handful," he said, shaking his head. "But she's doing great."

"What did you guys end up calling her?"

"Hazel."

The puppy in question was a lab-mix from a litter that had been dropped off at the Inn several weeks ago. The Chief and his wife had a Basset Hound named Wally who was a chronic howler when left alone in the house. We had suggested a second dog to keep him company, and they had agreed after giving the idea some serious thought.

"Hazel and Wally? It sounds like a sitcom from the sixties."

"Yeah, we're showing our age," the Chief said. "But it seems to be working. The neighbors haven't complained about Wally's howling since we got her. I think it was the perfect solution."

"Good," I said, coming to a stop.

He held my arm as I climbed into the boat and sat down behind the wheel. The Chief untied both lines then sat down next to me as I backed out of the slip. I headed for deep water at a leisurely pace and nodded at the backpack.

"There's a thermos of coffee in there," I said. "Can you pour me half a cup?"

"Half a cup?" Chief Abrams said, rummaging through the backpack.

"A cup and a half a day is my limit," I said, scanning the early morning horizon as I accepted the mug and took a sip.

"You want to try the same spot we did yesterday?"

"Sure," I said, angling the boat at a thirty-degree angle and accelerating. "It's nice to be out here."

"Yeah," he said, sipping coffee as he looked out at the water. "And it might be the last time we're able to do it. The weather is supposed to change this week for the worse."

"We're taking the boat out of the water next week," I said, then pondered the onset of winter and our decision not to go to the Cayman Islands. I must admit I had mixed emotions about the idea of spending the next four months dealing with the onslaught of cold and snow. "You know, Chief, just because we're staying here, it doesn't mean you guys shouldn't go. Our place down there is going to be empty most of the winter."

"Not a bad idea," the Chief said, then took a sip of coffee. "And I've got some vacation time I need to use."

"Just let me know," I said, making a left and heading upriver. "Oh, I meant to ask you about something."

"Shoot."

"When Josie and Chef Claire were in Italy, they spent a week at culinary school."

"And based on last night's dinner, we're all the better for it. What about it?"

"One of the students at the school turned out to be an undercover FBI agent."

"Yes, I know," he said, nodding. "Betty Smithsonian."

"That's her. How long have you known about her?"

"Awhile," Chief Abrams said. "The FBI guy in Washington thought I should be in the loop."

"Agent Tompkins?"

"Yeah, that's him. The one who's got the hots for Chef Claire."

"Josie and Chef Claire said Betty mentioned something about a smuggling ring operating in the area."

"Yeah," the Chief said, finishing the last of his coffee. "It's despicable."

"So, the rumors are true?"

"That they're smuggling people?" he said, glancing over at me. "Yeah."

"How much do you know about the details?"

"Not a lot," he said. "I'm sure the Feds know a lot more than they're willing to share, but I'm not surprised. They're not going to say much to a small-town cop."

"But they are definitely smuggling people?"

"No doubt about it," he said, shaking his head. "It makes you wonder about the human condition."

"You got that right. Let me guess, with all the extra attention being paid to the southern border, the smugglers decided to head north and come into the country from Canada?"

"That's what the Feds thought at first," the Chief said. "But that theory fell apart when they realized the logistics required to pull that off didn't make a lot of sense."

"They'd have to head north by boat to make that work," I said, nodding. "And if that's the case, why not just find a spot somewhere on either coast to drop them off, right?"

"Yeah, if they're able to pull that off, there's no reason to head all the way to Canada and then smuggle them back across the border. As soon as the Feds decided the people being brought in weren't coming from the south, they shifted their attention."

I glanced over at the Chief and waited for more.

"To the east," he said eventually.

"Let me guess," I said. "Eastern Europe."

"That the prevailing theory at the moment."

"Refugees?"

"That's what I thought at first," Chief Abrams said. "But Agent Tompkins has a different take."

"Well, if they aren't refugees, they must be people with money."

"Bingo."

"They're smuggling in rich people?"

"Not necessarily rich," the Chief said. "But definitely people who have enough money to pay for what they need."

"I'm going to need a bit more, Chief."

"That's where the details start to get a little fuzzy. But from what I was able to piece together, it sounds like the folks they're smuggling in are professionals and business people looking for a fresh start."

"So, these people are flying into Canada and then being smuggled across the border?" I said.

"No, it sounds like they're being brought into Canada by boat," the Chief said.

"I get it," I said, nodding. "They're crossing the ocean in cargo ships then heading up the Seaway."

"That's the working theory. When you think about it, it's pretty clever," the Chief said. "The ships crossing the Atlantic are huge. And all you need is a couple of containers onboard to move dozens of people."

"And since there are hundreds of containers on each ship, it would be like trying to find a needle in a haystack."

"It would," the Chief said, nodding. "And the haystack analogy only applies if you're actually looking for something. If human trafficking isn't on your radar, you wouldn't have a clue."

"And they're using our area to get them across the border."

"Ten minutes by boat and you can be in the good ole' USA."

"But why go to all that trouble?" I said. "If these people have money, why not just fly straight to Canada?"

"They're probably worried about being recognized at the airport," he said. "You know how closely authoritarian regimes watch their citizens. Especially the ones the government is already keeping track of."

"Wouldn't a private plane be an option?"

"I imagine it is for some people," Chief Abrams said. "But I'm pretty sure most governments track the comings and goings of private jets a lot closer than we might think."

"So, they slip undetected onto a ship," I said. "Yeah, I can make that work."

"They're definitely harder to track when they go by boat. And private planes are expensive. Most of them probably can't afford it given the other costs."

"New papers, right?" I said.

"Yeah. According to Agent Tompkins, they must be getting new identities as part of the package."

"Did he say how much it costs?"

"The Feds think it's a hundred thousand. Per person."

"Geez, nice work if you can get it, huh?" I said, shaking my head. "It sounds like the Feds have figured out a few things."

"They have a pretty good idea where the ships are originating out of, but they're still not clear how they're getting them across the border," the Chief said. "That's where Betty Smithsonian comes in."

"And you as well, right?"

"No, my involvement is on the periphery," he said. "All I'm doing is keeping an eye out for folks showing up in the town I don't know. Which is a lot easier now that tourist season is over."

"Have you seen anybody?"

"Not a one," the Chief said. "Agent Tompkins is convinced the smuggling ring is going to do one more run before winter gets here. So, we'll see." He shrugged. "But since there are hundreds of spots they could use for the drop-off, I don't like our chances. Especially if they do it at night."

"Have the Feds got other local police involved?" I said.

"I'm sure they do," he said. "Up and down the River. But the Feds are pretty sure it's happening around here."

"Dang it," I said, spotting a boat upriver from us. "Somebody is already fishing here."

24

"Probably Rooster," Chief Abrams said. "He's the one who told me about this spot."

"No, that's not Rooster's boat," I said as I pulled back on the throttle.

"You're right," he said. "Hang on, that's a Fish and Wildlife boat."

"They're already on their way to find the bear? They got an early start."

"They said they'd be heading out first thing in the morning. I guess they weren't kidding."

"Uh, Chief."

"What?"

"Unless my eyes are playing tricks on me, I don't see anybody on the boat."

Chapter 4

I put the boat in neutral, and Chief Abrams grabbed one side and tied the boats together. We both glanced around the twenty-foot runabout then frowned at each other.

"Weird," I said, glancing around the immediate stretch of water. "Where the heck did he go?"

"Well, it's a little cold for a swim," the Chief said, still frowning. "Maybe he fell in."

"But where?" I said, grabbing my binoculars and sweeping back and forth across the surface of the water.

"It has to be somewhere upriver. The current isn't that strong around here, but the boat is definitely drifting," the Chief said.

"They wouldn't have come out before first light, would they?"

"Doubtful," the Chief said, glancing out at the early morning sun. "It's been light for about an hour."

"Maybe he was running in the dark and hit something," I said, lowering the binoculars.

"That's possible," he said. "But I don't see any damage to the boat."

"So, what do you want to do?"

"Let's head upriver and take a look," the Chief said.

"Okay," I said, sitting back down behind the wheel.

"Just give me a sec," the Chief said, slowing making his way onto the Fish and Wildlife boat. He grabbed the boat's anchor and tossed it overboard then climbed back aboard. "That oughta hold it."

"You need to call anybody?" I said.

"Let's wait until we get a better idea of what might be going on. We'll know more in a few minutes," he said, sitting down next to me. "Let's do a slow cruise upriver until we hit Jackson's camp. We know that's where Fish and Wildlife was going."

"Yeah, it's not far from here," I said, accelerating. "Maybe they bought two boats."

"It's possible," the Chief said. "And maybe the other boat had some sort of cage for the bear."

I thought about it then frowned at him.

"And the Fish and Wildlife agents both left on the same boat," he said without much conviction. "But they didn't do a good job of securing the other boat."

"I suppose," I said with a shrug.

"But you're not buying it?"

"It sounds like a bit of a stretch, Chief."

"Yeah, it kinda does," he said, rubbing his forehead.

Minutes later, we caught a glimpse of Jackson's cabin nestled amid a stand of pines. I slowed to a crawl, and both of us scanned the shoreline. Coming up empty, I focused on the small structure then frowned. The Chief caught the look on my face.

"What is it?"

"Take a look," I said, pointing at the cabin. "What's odd about this picture?"

"Huh, what do you know?" the Chief said. "Did Jackson say anything about staying at his camp?"

"No, you heard him," I said, staring at the smoke rising above the pines. "He's way too busy at the store."

"Maybe he's giving the new owner a tour of the place," the Chief said, getting to his feet.

"Maybe."

"I see four boats at the three docks. Plus, there's two in the boathouse. Who else has a camp on the island?"

"There are at least four different families," I said. "But I think they're all seasonal folks and gone for the year."

"Why are their boats still in the water?"

"I imagine they hire locals to handle it. Probably haven't gotten around to taking them out yet."

"That makes sense," he said, grabbing the edge of the dock. He tied the boat off then climbed out. "I'm going to check on the cabin. You stay here with the boat, okay?"

"Why?"

"Because you're pregnant and I don't have a clue what we might be dealing with," he said.

"Oh, come on, Chief," I said. "You're such a worrywart."

"No, stay here and wait for me, Suzy. Stay."

"Woof."

28

"Funny."

"Well, if you're going to talk to me like I'm a dog, the least I can do is act like one."

"Just stay with the boat, okay. I'll be right back. And while you're here, why don't you keep checking the water for signs of our missing Fish and Wildlife agent?"

"I can do that," I said, mildly miffed. Then I spotted my backpack. "Maybe I'll have a snack while you're gone."

"There you go," he said. "Just hang tight. I won't be long."

I watched him head down the dock then up the path that led to the cabin a couple hundred feet away. Smoke continued to rise from the chimney as a strong gust of wind out of the north whipped the pines.

"If I were staying here, I'd certainly have a fire going," I said to myself as I reached for a bag of granola. "Jackson must have given the key to a friend."

Then I remembered the bear cub and the hairs on the back of my neck rose. I glanced around and spotted a less-exposed dock nearby. I untied the boat and idled into the slip about a hundred feet away. I secured the boat and turned the engine off. I grabbed my binoculars and scanned up and down the River several times before giving up. I set the binoculars down and stretched out on the seat running along the transom and closed my eyes.

I drifted off and dreamt of bear cubs waterskiing behind speedboats being driving by their mama before waking with a start. I glanced around, momentarily confused about where I was. I checked my watch and realized I'd been asleep for half an hour. Concerned, I grabbed my binoculars and scanned the cabin and surrounding woods. My search came up empty, and I decided the Chief was either chatting with the people staying in the cabin or was in some sort of trouble. Putting aside all thoughts about the bear cub and the possibility it was traveling with one or both of its parents, I climbed out of the boat and walked down the dock.

I began a slow walk up the inclined path and scanned the area for signs of the bear cub. I got halfway before I heard the voices of two men. Since neither one was the Chief's, I left the path and did my best lumber into the nearby pines. I crouched down behind a large boulder and groaned when my body protested.

"Did you hear something?"

"No, I didn't hear nothin'. Probably just the wind."

I frowned when I recognized one of the voices. But I couldn't put a face or name to it. I sat down with my back against the boulder and cocked my head as I strained to hear the conversation.

"Give me the keys. It's my turn to drive."

"You drove yesterday."

"Did not. Give me the keys."

"Pound sand."

Now, the question of who owned the familiar voice was officially stuck in my head and tormenting me like an itch you can't scratch. I was momentarily distracted from the question when I realized my heart was pounding. I focused on my breathing and made myself as small as possible behind the boulder.

"Good luck with that," I whispered to myself, then giggled.

"You must have heard that."

"I tell you it's just the wind," the unfamiliar voice said.

"You sure it's okay to leave the cop there with no one watching him?"

"How do you know he's a cop?"

"I recognize him from the last time I was here," the familiar voice said. "He's the chief of police in Clay Bay."

"Where's he going to go? He's tied to a damn chair. If I were you, I'd be more worried about the one from Fish and Wildlife turning up."

"She's long gone," the familiar voice said.

"Are you sure you hit her?"

"Of course, I'm sure. You saw the way she went under."

"I did. But are you sure you saw her?"

"You're a funny guy, Roger. A real hoot."

"What if somebody else shows up while we're gone?"

"Don't worry. Wilbur will take care of anybody who happens to drop by."

Both men laughed, and I heard their footsteps on the gravel.

31

"Hey, hold on," the familiar voice said.

The footsteps stopped, and I froze when I realized how close they were.

"What's the matter?"

"There's an extra boat at the dock."

"You idiot. Of course, there is. Do you think the cop walked here?"

"Oh, right," the familiar voice said. "Should we do the same thing we did with the Fish and Wildlife boat?"

"No, let's leave it there for now. One empty boat found floating is one thing. But two showing up on the same day is just going to get people asking a lot of questions."

"Makes sense. Now, give me those keys."

"Bite me."

"Then I'm driving back later."

"We'll see."

They resumed their walk, and I waited until I heard them reach the dock. I peered out from behind the boulder then cursed myself for leaving the binoculars in the boat. Moments later, I heard the engine roar as they sped away from the dock. As soon as the sound of the boat faded, I picked up the throaty hum of a generator running somewhere in the distance. I stood up and glanced around for signs of the mysterious Wilbur. In all likelihood, he was armed and dangerous. Eschewing the path, I slowly made my way through the stretch of pines toward the cabin.

Given the elevated porch, it was impossible to get a good look inside without revealing my presence, so I headed for the back of the cabin. I slowly worked my way along one side, my shoulder brushing the exterior wall. When I reached the back of the cabin, I came to another porch. I paused to catch my breath and get a better feel for my surroundings. I'd only been to Jackson's camp a few times, and my memory was sketchy. A garden, showing serious signs of late-fall fatigue, ran along the back of the property. A corrugated tin storage shed sat about twenty feet from the cabin, and I remembered it was where Jackson kept his tools and firewood.

I was about to make my way up the back steps when I spotted the bear cub rummaging through what was left of the garden. Then I heard a noise coming from inside the cabin. Momentarily frozen in my tracks, I panicked then made a beeline for the storage shed.

The bear also heard the noise and turned around. When it saw me doing my best lumber across the lawn, it dropped what was left of the pumpkin it had in its mouth and bared its teeth. Against my better judgment, I stopped and stared in disbelief at the animal. What I had assumed was a bear cub was actually an enormous Tibetan Mastiff. Close to three feet tall and weighing in at what had to be two hundred pounds, the dog continued to bare its teeth as it emitted a low, deep guttural growl that made the hairs on the back of my neck tingle.

"You must be Wilbur," I said as calmly as I could manage.

The massive dog, displaying considerable speed and agility, dashed across the lawn heading straight for me. I forced myself to run and reached the storage shed in half a dozen steps. I frantically worked the door halfway open and squeezed myself inside. I pulled the door shut with assistance from the Mastiff who had hurled himself through the air and slammed into the door with his front paws. The impact knocked me back, and I groaned when I landed on a chunk of firewood.

The dog, undeterred, began trying to get the door open as he continued his deep growl. I scrambled on my hands and knees and pulled the door shut. I continued to hold it closed until I located the light switch, then the door latch. Satisfied the door was secure, I glanced around the shed now bathed in light. The dirt floor was dominated by firewood and a riding lawn mower. Various tools hung on hooks, and I spotted a few gaps where the corrugated tin walls met the ground.

The growls were now interspersed with barking as the Mastiff continued to paw at the front door. Then the Mastiff fell silent. I listened closely and eventually realized the dog was circling the perimeter of the storage shed.

"Wilbur, are you stalking me?" I finally managed.

The dog resumed his low, guttural growl as he continued to circle the shed.

"Wilbur? Who's the good boy, huh?"

A round of loud barks followed, and I shook my head as I sat down on the riding lawnmower. I reached into my coat pocket, searching for my phone. Coming up empty, I checked the pockets of my shirt and jeans. Then I remembered I'd left my phone in its charger on the boat.

"Crap."

Chapter 5

A few minutes later, Wilbur refocused on getting the door open. I leaned against the wall and snuck a peek outside through a small gap. The dog was on his belly and using his front paws to bend the bottom of the door back. When he made enough progress, he began chewing on the bottom of the wood frame. I heard a chunk of wood break off, and I saw the dog toss the piece away with a flick of his head. He growled and barked a few more times before resuming his attack on the door.

"C'mon, Wilbur. Let's be friends, okay?"

The dog barked and snapped his jowls then went back to work.

"Fine. Have it your way."

I took another look around the shed for something I could use to defend myself. The last thing I'd ever want to do would be to hurt a dog, but if it came down to a choice between the dog and the safety of my baby, it would be an easy decision. But hopefully, it wouldn't come to that. I relaxed when the dog stopped working on the door and resumed his stalking of the perimeter.

If I could come up with a good distraction to shift the dog's attention in a different direction, I might have time to make my way onto the back porch. But if the back door was locked, I knew I'd be in serious trouble if I got trapped by the dog before I could figure out a way to get inside. Then I realized Wilbur had started pawing at one of the gaps between the corrugated tin and dirt floor. I heard the dog digging and soon saw his front paws emerge. The hairs on the back of my neck rose again, and I shook my head at the dog's determination.

"Tenacious little thing, aren't you?"

The dog barked several times in rapid succession before resuming his frantic attempt to dig a hole big enough for him to crawl under and get at me.

"They should have called you Cujo, Wilbur."

The dog seemed to disagree and let loose with another round of guttural growls. I took another look around the shed for something to use to protect myself in case the dog didn't hit any rocky resistance on his dig. Then I froze when I heard a soft knock on the door.

"Hello?" I whispered.

"Open the door," a woman whispered back.

It was impossible to miss the urgency in her voice, but I still wasn't convinced Wilbur hadn't added English to his skill set. I glanced at the dog who was still intensely focused on tunneling his way in.

"Who is it?" I whispered.

"Just open the damn door before the dog realizes I'm standing out here."

I slowly pushed the door partway open, and a young, uniformed woman worked her way inside the shed. I pulled the door shut and latched it then focused on the woman who was soaked and shivering. Moments later, I realized she was also bleeding from the shoulder.

"Geez, are you all right?"

"What do you think?" she snapped, then softened. "Sorry. Thanks for letting me in. I've been hiding from the dog. I'm Jennifer. Jennifer Johnson. I'm with Fish and Wildlife."

"What on earth happened to you?" I said, looking around the shed for something she might be able to wear.

"I got shot, then almost drowned," she said.

I spotted a large cloth tarp used to collect lawn trimmings and grabbed it off the wall.

"You need to get out of those clothes," I said, shaking as much dirt and grass as I could off the tarp.

"Good call," she said, unbuttoning her blouse with her good arm. "But I'm going to need some help."

I helped her out of her uniform and draped the tarp over her shoulders. She continued to shake and shiver. I took another look around and spotted a pair of men's overalls hanging from a hook. I grabbed them, shook them out the best I could then helped her out of the tarp and into the overalls. I draped the tarp around her again and took a look at the baggy ensemble and smiled.

"You look like a homeless superhero."

"A cold, homeless superhero," she said, clutching herself with her good arm.

"Probably not what you'd wear on a first date, but it's going to have to do."

"I'll forgo fashion for the moment," she said, managing a small smile before she winced and pressed a hand against her wounded shoulder. "Geez, that hurts."

We both glanced at the gap in the wall when Wilbur's front legs reached halfway through.

"What a beast," Jennifer said. "You think we can make it to the cabin before he catches up to us?"

"I don't like our chances," I said. "I'm surprised you took the risk."

"It was either that or freeze to death," she said, flinching when the dog's legs made even more progress. "What are we going to do? I can't imagine doing anything to hurt an animal. But I might have to make an exception."

"His name is Wilbur."

"You know the dog?"

"No, we just met," I said, staring at the dog's relentless digging. "But he is beautiful."

"We must have a different definition," Jennifer said. "I need to get inside that cabin."

"Me too. My friend is in there."

"Yeah, I saw him go in. I was about to follow him when those two morons let the dog out. That was when I headed to the woods to hide."

"I can't wait to hear your story," I said, keeping a close eye on the dog's progress. "But we need to figure a way out of here before Wilbur joins the party."

"Yeah, he's a digger, isn't he?"

"Indeed. And probably also a biter," I said.

"You want to make a run for it?" Jennifer said, glancing at the door.

"I don't think we can outrun him," I said, shaking my head.

"I've only got to outrun you," she said with a grin.

"Funny. Everybody's a comedian," I said, then spotted something sitting on a workbench. "Hang on. I've got an idea."

I headed for the workbench and grabbed a long strap with a plastic buckle on one end. I held it up for her to see.

"What is that?"

"My guess is Jackson uses it to secure supplies and groceries he brings over here."

"Jackson?"

"A friend of mine who owns the place," I said, then focused on the dog's front legs. "If you think you can manage it with one arm, I need you to grab one of the dog's legs. I'll get the other, and if we can get the strap tied around his legs, we should have enough time to get into the cabin before he chews through it."

"Should have enough time?"

40

"It's the best I got at the moment," I said with a shrug. "What do you say?"

"Okay, let's do it," she said, heading for the gap in the wall and kneeling down next to one of Wilbur's frantically digging legs.

I knelt on the opposite side of her and got the strap ready.

"He's gonna get cranky as soon as we grab his legs."

"Yeah, I kinda figured that," Jennifer said, wincing. "And to think I was worried about having to deal with a bear cub this morning."

"On three," I said, firmly planting my knees in the dirt.

I counted in a whisper, and we each grabbed a leg. The Mastiff growled and barked as he tried to pull his legs back. But he didn't have the leverage he needed, and we pressed his legs together. I wrapped the strap around the dog's legs at the joint several times in rapid succession, then secured the buckle and pulled the strap tight. The dog continued to snarl and bark.

"Well done," Jennifer said, brushing herself off as she got to her feet. "I assume you've done this before."

"He's not my first problem dog. Let's go."

"Lead the way."

I pushed the door open, and we headed for the cabin. I snuck a peek over my shoulder at the dog who had managed to get his legs out from underneath the shed. He was already gnawing at the strap and appeared to be making short work of it.

We climbed the short set of steps, and I reached for the doorknob.

"Please," I said, glancing skyward as I turned the knob. "Don't be locked."

The door opened easily with a soft squeak, and we entered the cabin and closed the door behind us. I immediately headed through the kitchen and into the living room where I spotted the Chief with a bag over his head. His arms and legs were bound to a chair with duct tape.

"See if you can find a sharp knife."

I made my way to the chair and removed the bag from the Chief's head. He gave me a wild-eyed stare. I slowly removed the strip of duct tape from his mouth, and he flinched as it gave way.

"It's about time," he finally managed to get out.

"You're welcome. We were dealing with a rather tenacious beast outside."

"I heard a dog but didn't get a look at him," the Chief said. "Hang on. We?"

"You'll see," I said, examining the tape wrapped around his hands.

Jennifer returned brandishing a large knife. The Chief stared at her wild look and the tarp draped over her shoulders.

"I sure hope she's with you," he said, frowning.

"This is Jennifer," I said. "She's with Fish and Wildlife. Jennifer, this is Chief Abrams."

"Nice to meet you," she said, expertly slicing through the duct tape.

The Chief massaged his hands, then slowly got to his feet.

"Are you okay?" I said, giving him a quick once-over.

"Apart from my pride being wounded," he said. "I can't believe I let those two get the jump on me."

"Do you know who they are?" I said. "I recognized one of their voices, but couldn't put my finger on it."

"No, I didn't get a look at them. As soon as I stepped inside, they grabbed me, duct-taped my mouth and put the bag over my head."

Jennifer tossed the tarp aside and headed for the fireplace. She stood with her back close to the fire and hugged herself for warmth with her good arm.

"Hey, I see blood on your overalls," the Chief said, approaching her.

"Yeah, I got shot in the shoulder."

"Let me take a look," he said, gently unsnapping the top two buttons and pulling the fabric back. "We need to get you to the hospital. Let's hit the road."

"Hang on," I said, looking out one of the windows where the Mastiff was already back to full strength. "Geez, he chewed through the strap already."

"That was fast," Jennifer said. "No way I'm going back out there until we have some sort of plan to deal with him."

"Can't argue with your logic," I said, taking another look at the dog who was climbing the steps. His teeth were bared, and he began pacing the back porch.

"What's he doing?" Jennifer said.

"Looking for someone to focus his wrath on," I said, shaking my head at the enormous beast. I left the window and sat down in a chair near the fire. "I knew Mastiffs were territorial, but this guy has raised it to an art form."

"We need to call somebody," the Chief said.

"My phone's in the boat," I said.

"Mine's in the water," Jennifer said.

"Well, that's not good," the Chief said, then focused on Jennifer. "How did you end up getting shot?"

"Beats the heck out of me," she said, sitting down. "I got here early this morning to check out a report of a bear cub on the island."

"That was me," the Chief said. "We were driving by yesterday around sunset and saw it sitting on the dock. At least, at the time we thought it was a bear."

"I understand your confusion," Jennifer said. "I was asked to confirm the sighting then call the folks who handle capture and relocation."

"But you didn't get the chance?" I said.

"No, as soon as I pulled into the dock, a guy approached me before I could even get out of the boat. He freaked out and yelled that the cops were here. He must have seen my Fish and Wildlife uniform and assumed I was with the police. Then he pulled a gun on me. Another guy ran down to the dock, and they started arguing with each other about how the guy with the gun was always overreacting."

"You don't know who they were, do you?" the Chief said.

"Not a clue," Jennifer said, shaking her head. "As soon as their argument heated up, I hit the throttle and got the heck out of there. But they followed and caught up about a quarter mile downriver. That's when the guy shot me."

"Just like that?" the Chief said.

"Yeah," she said, nodding. "The impact knocked me in the water, and the idiot kept shooting. So, I kept diving deeper and eventually made my way into a section of marsh. If it hadn't been so early in the morning, I'm sure they would have found me and finished the job."

"You're very lucky," I said. "And smart."

"Thanks," she said. "But I don't feel smart at the moment. Why do you think they panicked like that?"

The Chief fell silent for a long time. Eventually, the penny dropped, and I stared back at him.

"The smuggling ring," I whispered.

"That's exactly what I was thinking."

"But why would they be operating out of Jackson's camp?" I said.

"A very good question."

"Smuggling ring?" Jennifer said.

"Yes," the Chief said. "There's one rumored to be operating around here."

"Smuggling what?"

"People," the Chief said.

"What?"

"Yeah, I know," the Chief said, glancing out a window. "Man, he is a bruiser, isn't he?"

"What's he doing?"

"Licking his chops, I think. We've gotta figure a way out of here. Jennifer needs to see a doctor."

"Yeah," I said, getting up to stand close to the fire. "Did you get a good look at the guys?"

"Close enough to recognize them if our paths cross again," she said. "One, obviously the smarter of the pair, was short with dark hair and a beard. The other one, the idiot, was a big guy with one unmistakable characteristic."

"What was that?" the Chief said.

"He had the thickest lenses in his glasses I've ever seen."

The Chief and I stared at each other.

"Is it possible?" he said.

"It has to be him, right?" I said, frowning.

"But Rooster told him in no uncertain terms, if he ever came back here, he'd end up at the bottom of the River."

"He's always proven himself to be a slow learner," I said.

"I know. But still," the Chief said.

"Who are you talking about?" Jennifer said, glancing back and forth at us.

"Coke Bottle," we said in unison.

Chapter 6

Coke Bottle was Rooster's cousin whose actual name was Walter. But when we got our first look at his glasses, we'd given him the nickname, and it had stuck. He was an infamous local criminal we'd crossed paths with twice in the past. On second thought, putting him in the same category as other thieves and grifters gave criminals a bad name. And it wasn't so much *what* he did since Clay Bay has a long history of people who exhibit criminal behavior yet continue to live among us in relative harmony. It was *how* Coke Bottle conducted his activities that separated him from his brethren. He was stupid, stubborn and sullen, and cursed with terrible eyesight that made simple activities, like watching television, extremely difficult. I use the television reference instead of reading since I'm pretty sure the only time Coke Bottle picked up a book was to kill a bug.

The fact he was back in the area was surprising. He'd been banished after our last encounter when we'd caught him trying to steal the semen of a rare and valuable Tibetan Mastiff in Pennsylvania. Judging by the beast continuing to circle the cabin, Coke Bottle had figured out a way to keep some of the spoils for his own purposes. Or, more likely, he'd managed to steal one of the breeder's adult dogs. His banishment wasn't delivered by the authorities; it came via his cousin. And to put it mildly, Rooster hadn't given Coke Bottle the news of his banishment verbally. It was delivered in, let's call it, a more forceful manner.

I studied the look on the Chief's face, a look similar to mine I was sure.

"I can't believe he had the guts to come back here."

"Yeah, Rooster's going to go ballistic when he hears the news," the Chief said.

"Who is this guy?" Jennifer said, continuing to gently hold her injured shoulder.

"Blind reprobate is probably the kindest term I can use," the Chief said, peering out through the front window.

"Any sign of them coming back?" I said, glancing around the cabin.

"Not yet," the Chief said, stepping away from the window. "But we need to figure a way out of here. We have to get Jennifer's wound looked at."

"I can wait," Jennifer said, forcing a laugh. "There's no way I'm going out there with that beast on the loose."

"Me either," I said, then nodded as an idea emerged. "We should let the dog in."

"Now that's funny," the Chief said with a grin. The smile disappeared when he saw the look on my face. "Hang on. You're not joking, are you?"

"No, we need to get him in here and make sure he can't get out," I said, surveying the cabin.

"I'm going to need a bit more, Suzy," the Chief said.

"There's a back bedroom off the kitchen," I said. "Follow me."

I headed into the kitchen and crossed the room until I reached the bedroom.

"We're in luck," I said, staring at the bedroom door. "It closes from the kitchen."

"And that matters why?" Jennifer said, frowning.

"Because if it closed from the bedroom side, my plan wouldn't work," I said with a shrug.

"Are you always this cryptic?" Jennifer said.

"Yeah, I should probably start working on that."

"Okay, Snoopmeister," the Chief said, leaning against the kitchen counter. "Lay it on me."

"When we let him in, he's going to go after whatever crosses his path."

"Let's make sure it's not us," Jennifer said. "He's going to tear into the first thing he sees."

"Absolutely," I said. "We just need to make sure the dog goes after the first thing he *hears*."

"Again, I'm not following you," Jennifer said.

"A simple distraction," I said. "One of us needs to stand behind the door out of sight."

"Which one?" Jennifer said, scowling at the idea.

"That would be me," Chief Abrams said. "If we decide to go down that path. But first, if you don't mind, I'd like to hear the rest of your plan."

"I'll stand on the kitchen table over there," I said, nodding at the far wall. "It's out of the dog's initial line of sight. As soon as the dog comes in, I'll throw something into the bedroom. Something that's going to make a lot of noise when it hits the floor."

"And the dog follows the noise into the bedroom and I slam the door behind him," the Chief said, nodding.

"Exactly. And then we depart at our leisure," I said.

"But before he chews through the door, right?" Jennifer said.

"Yeah," I said, then frowned when another thought came to mind.

"What's the matter?" the Chief said.

"Does the door have a doorknob or a latch on the bedroom side?"

"It's a doorknob on both sides," he said.

"Good. He'd be able to open a latch in about ten seconds," I said.

"That's your plan?" Jennifer said.

"Unless you've got a better idea," I said.

"I saw a shotgun hanging over the fireplace," she said. "Wouldn't it be easier to shoot the dog?"

"We're not shooting the dog," I said as a simple statement of fact. "He's only following his instincts. And the fact he hasn't been socialized isn't his fault. The blame for that lies at the feet of Coke Bottle."

"Then we'll shoot Coke Bottle," the Chief said with a shrug.

"Not the worst idea you've had today, Chief."

"I still think we need protection," Jennifer said. "What if you miss with your throw and the dog ends up staying in the kitchen?"

I thought about the question then conceded the point.

"It's a possibility," I said.

"Are you athletic?" Jennifer said.

"You're new here, aren't you?" the Chief said to her, then laughed.

"Shut it."

"Tell you what," the Chief said. "I'll hold the shotgun." Then he saw the look on my face and held both palms up to calm me. "But I will only use it on the dog as a last resort."

"And then only in the leg," I said, staring at him. "Got it?"

"Got it," the Chief said. "Okay, let's do this. What are you going to throw?"

I glanced around the kitchen then headed for one of the cabinets.

"Perfect," I said, grabbing the metal lid from one of the pots. "This thing is basically a metal Frisbee. That I can handle."

"And it's certainly going to make a racket when it hits the floor," the Chief said.

"Okay," I said, heading for the kitchen table. I climbed up then held the lid in my outstretched arm. "I should probably take a practice throw."

"Go for it," the Chief said.

I fired the lid across the kitchen, and it landed near the door and bounced into the bedroom. The dog immediately began growling and barking, and he scratched hard and fast against the outside wall.

"Wow," Jennifer said. "That certainly got his attention. I think this just might work."

"All I need to do now is repeat the throw," I said, heading to the bedroom to retrieve the lid. "Jennifer, you might want to wait in the other bedroom with the door closed. There's no need to put you in jeopardy."

"Says the woman who's pregnant," Jennifer said.

"Oh, you noticed," I said, patting my belly. "I didn't think I was showing through this outfit."

"A bit," she said. "How far along are you?"

"Almost five months. Eighteen weeks, actually."

"Congratulations," she said.

"Thanks," I said, climbing back up on the table.

"I'll get the shotgun," the Chief said, heading for the living room before returning moments later. "Okay, I'm ready to go."

"Only in the leg as a last resort, Chief," I said.

"I'll do my best," the Chief said, taking up his position behind the door.

"Only in the leg," I said firmly. "Jennifer, is the dog still standing outside the bedroom window?"

"He is."

"Okay, open the back door then lock yourself in the other bedroom," I said.

"Be careful," she said, slowly opening the door before scurrying out of the kitchen.

"You're ready, Chief?"

"I am," he said from behind the door.

"Good," I said. "Because this will probably play out fast."

"Let's do it."

I whistled loudly and soon heard the dog's nails on the steps. Moments later, his head emerged, and I tossed the metal lid through the air. It landed with a *clang*, and the Tibetan snarled as he scrambled across the linoleum fighting for traction. The dog disappeared from sight after entering the bedroom.

"Close it," I shouted.

The Chief slammed the door shut and moments later the dog let loose with an impressive string of snarls and barks as he scratched violently at the door. I climbed down off the table and gave the Chief two thumbs up.

"Well done," I said.

"Nice throw," he said. "Okay, let's get the heck out of here."

He collected Jennifer from her hiding place, and all three of us left via the back door, checking twice to make sure it was closed tight. We made our way down the path to the dock and scanned the water for other boats. Seeing none, he helped both of us into the boat then untied the lines and hopped in. I climbed in and fired up the engine. I backed out of the slip then pressed the throttle hard.

"How are you doing?" I said to Jennifer who was sitting next to me holding her shoulder.

"I'll be fine," she said. "What a day. And to think I joined Fish and Wildlife instead of the state police to eliminate the chance of getting shot."

"People plan, God laughs," I said, grinning at her.

"Yeah," she said, nodding. "It's always something, right?"

"I need to call the hospital," the Chief said as he grabbed his phone. "This is Chief Abrams. I'm going to need medical assistance at the front dock in about fifteen minutes. I'm bringing in a female with a gunshot wound to the shoulder. Yes, I can hold." He glanced back and forth at us. "The receptionist is getting Doc Jones."

"Don't forget to clarify things, Chief," I said, staring at him.

"What?" he said, confused. Then the penny dropped. "Oh, right. Silly me. Hey, Doc. Chief Abrams here…Yeah, it's a shoulder wound. She's conscious and it looks like the bleeding has stopped. But she's probably going to need a pint or two…Okay, hang on." The Chief looked at Jennifer. "You wouldn't happen to know your blood type by any chance?"

"O-positive."

"That makes it a bit easier," the Chief said. "She's O-positive, Doc. Oh, before I go, make sure you let Mrs. C. know that the victim isn't Suzy." Then the Chief laughed. "Yeah, that wouldn't be good for any of us. Okay, we'll see you in about ten."

"Thanks, Chief," I said after he put his phone away.

"How mad do you think she's going to be?"

"Hard to tell," I said, shrugging. "Probably somewhere between unbridled hostility and ballistic."

"Sorry to get you involved in this," the Chief said.

"It wasn't your fault," I said, pressing the throttle down all the way. "It wasn't anybody's fault. That might be the only thing that saves us."

"I doubt it," he said.

"Who are you talking about?" Jennifer shouted above the roar of the engine.

"My mother."

"Sure, I get that," Jennifer said. "If my pregnant daughter got involved in a situation like this, I'd be furious."

"Whose side are you on?" I said, then grinned at the Chief.

"Gunshots and a vicious dog trying to take our face off?" Jennifer said. "She's got every right to be upset."

"Do me a favor, Jennifer," I said, glancing over at her.

"What's that?"

"Let me tell the story."

Chapter 7

Rooster stared at me in disbelief then focused on Chief Abrams who nodded in agreement. Rooster tossed back the last of his B&B. He gently set the glass down on the table and took several slow, deep breaths.

"Are you sure it's him?" he said eventually.

"Neither one of us saw him," the Chief said. "But the description fits him perfectly."

"I'm sure it does," Rooster said. "How many blind idiots who haven't made a smart decision in their life do you know?"

"Hard to argue with your logic," I said, taking a sip of my fizzy water.

"And he has a Mastiff?"

"Yeah, he must have gone back to that breeder's place in Pennsylvania," I said. "He's a beautiful dog."

The Chief snorted and shook his head.

"Beautiful?"

"He was just doing what he was bred to do," I whispered.

"I guess," the Chief said, then looked at Rooster. "The dog has to weigh two hundred pounds."

"What the heck is he doing back in the area?" Rooster said.

"We do have a theory," the Chief said.

"I gotta hear this," Rooster said, waving to Millie behind the bar for another drink.

"We think he might be involved with a smuggling ring that's operating around here," the Chief said.

"Smuggling?" Rooster said, frowning. "Well, that's right up Walter's alley. What are they bringing across the River?"

"People," I said.

"What?"

"Yeah, despicable, huh?" I said. "It looks like Eastern Europeans with money are being smuggled across the Atlantic then up the River."

"Walter's not smart enough to handle something like that on his own," Rooster said.

"No, he's not," the Chief said. "But an operation like that needs someone who knows the River. And some muscle work done from time to time."

"That he can handle," Rooster said. "I can't believe he had the cojones to come back here. I thought I made it perfectly clear the last time I saw him his presence wasn't welcome."

"Obviously a slow learner," I said, glancing at the door when it opened. I waved to Jackson and he immediately headed for us.

"I'll just have to make sure he gets the message this time," Rooster said, then beamed at Millie when she arrived with his drink. "Thanks, Millie."

"You're welcome," she said, glancing around. "Can I get you guys anything else?"

"No, I'm good," I said. "Thanks."

"I could use another glass of wine," the Chief said, then tossed back what was left in his glass.

"You got it," Millie said. "Hey, Jackson. Long time, no see. What can I get you?"

"Whatever wine the Chief is drinking will be fine. Thanks."

Jackson took a few moments to warm his hands in front of the fire then sat down next to me on the couch. He glanced around and frowned at our expressions.

"Okay, I'm here," Jackson said, then focused on Chief Abrams. "You said you had something important to talk about."

"We do," the Chief said. "We had an interesting encounter at your camp today."

"At my camp? I've had the place closed up since early October. What happened?"

"You have a couple of visitors staying there," the Chief said. "Or at least you did. I imagine they've cleared out by now."

"Who is it?" Jackson said, thoroughly confused.

"Well, for one, my cousin," Rooster said.

"Your cousin?" Jackson said, then frowned. "Not that idiot, Coke Bottle?"

"That's the one," I said.

"Has he ever been there before?" the Chief said.

"I think he tagged along on one of our fishing trips several years ago," Jackson said. "And we all ended up staying the night. Yeah, I remember. He was definitely there. He was afraid of the thunder and lightning."

"That would be Walter," Rooster said.

"What the heck are they doing at my camp?" Jackson said.

"We're not sure," the Chief said, giving me his best *keep quiet* look. "But we think he might be involved in something illegal."

"Geez, Chief," Jackson said, then laughed. "What are the odds?"

"Yeah. I just wanted to check with you and make sure you hadn't given him permission to be there."

"Give me a little credit, Chief. I know Walter. Not a chance in hell I would do that," Jackson said. "Hey, is this somehow related to the shooting of a Fish and Wildlife agent today?"

"It is," the Chief said. "She was shot on her boat then made her way back to your place."

"Is she going to be okay?"

"Yeah, they patched her up, and she was released this afternoon," the Chief said. "She'll be off work for a while, but she's going to be fine. She was lucky. In fact, Suzy probably saved her life. Mine too."

"I wouldn't go that far," I said, waving it off.

"Hey, if the shoe fits," the Chief said, then focused on Jackson. "Okay, I'll let you know as soon as I learn more. But

61

you might want to head over there tomorrow and check things out. I'm happy to go with you if you want."

"No, that's okay, Chief. Actually, I need to head over to camp with the guy who's buying the store. He wants to get a look at the cabin before making his final decision."

"Just be on the lookout," the Chief said. "I'm almost positive they're gone, but if you see any signs they're still there, just leave and give me a call right away."

"Will do," Jackson said, then glanced over at me. "What's the special tonight?"

"Chef Claire has a couple of stews with salad. And don't forget to try the new bread," I said.

"Ah, yes," Jackson said. "The mysterious rustic Italian loaf everyone is talking about."

"You won't believe how good it is," Rooster said. "Damn. I can't believe that idiot is back in town."

"Any idea where he might have gone?" I said.

"Nah," he said, shaking his head. "There are dozens of places where he could be hiding. Walter's spent a lot of time on the River and knows his way around."

The front door of the restaurant slowly opened and my mother entered. She smiled at the hostess and removed her coat and handed it over. Then she took a couple of steps forward and looked around the bar and lounge. When she spotted me sitting near the fire, she put her hands on her hips and gave me a gunslinger's glare that would have made Billy the Kid proud.

"It doesn't look like she's packing," I said. "That's a good sign."

"Don't make me laugh," the Chief said, biting his lip. "Geez, she's running hot."

My mother slowly approached, her laser-like stare never leaving my eyes. She sat down across from me, then looked around and nodded.

"Good evening, gentlemen," she said.

"Hi, Mrs. C.," Jackson said. "How are you doing?"

"I'll let you know," she said, again glaring at me. "Jackson, if you and Rooster would be so kind to give us a minute. I need to have a word with my daughter."

"We'll be in the dining room," Rooster said, getting to his feet and nodding for Jackson to follow him.

"I think I'll join you," the Chief said, starting to get up out of his chair.

"You stay right there, Chief," my mother said, maintaining her focus on me.

"Okay," he said, sitting back down and reaching for his wine glass.

My mother motioned to Millie she'd like a drink then casually draped a leg over her knee.

"Hello, darling. How was your day?"

"Trick question, right?"

"Don't even think about getting cute with me, young lady."

"Sorry, Mom."

"Tell me what happened," she said, glancing up when Millie arrived carrying a glass of wine. "Thanks, Millie." She took a small sip and gently set the glass on the table. "All of it, from the beginning."

"Geez, Mom," I said, frowning. "Lighten up. It was just one of those things."

"Start talking, young lady."

I did. As I talked, the Chief occasionally jumped in to provide additional details or confirm what I was telling her. My mother listened closely without interrupting, and when I finished, I sat back and waited for her reaction.

"Okay," she said, slowly nodding her head. "It's clear you didn't go looking for trouble."

"I did not."

"And it sounds like you were quite brave."

"She was," the Chief said. "And she saved the agent's life as well as mine."

"I don't know about that," I said. "But everything turned out fine, Mom."

My mother exhaled audibly as if she'd sprung a small leak. Then she stood and reached out to give me a hug. Surprised, I returned the embrace and frowned at her as she sat back down and took a sip of wine.

"That's it?" I said.

"What would you like me to do, darling."

64

"Nothing. I just expected to be harangued."

"Harangued?" my mother said, raising an eyebrow at me. "Don't push your luck, young lady."

"Got it, Mom. So, how was your day?"

"Not good," she said with a frown. "I thought we'd found the perfect doctor to replace Dr. Jefferson, but she decided not to take the job. We're back to square one."

"I'm sorry, Mom. I know how hard you've been working on it."

"It's taking forever," she said. "What's your take on why that horrible man is back in town, Chief?"

"We think he might be involved with a smuggling ring operating in the area," Chief Abrams said.

"Which one?"

"Which one?" I said. "Geez, Mom. How many do you know about?"

"Darling, people have been smuggling all sorts of contraband across the River forever. I'm sure the practice continues pretty much unabated."

"This one deals with smuggling people," the Chief said.

"People?" my mother said, shaking her head. "That's disgusting. Do you know what sort of role Rooster's cousin is playing?"

"Given his background and overall personality, our best guess is he helps the people running the operation with navigating the River. And I imagine he provides muscle when needed," the Chief said.

"What are you doing to catch them?" my mother said.

"Well, the FBI has asked all the local cops up and down the River to keep an eye out," the Chief said.

"But it's a tough nut to crack," I said. "There's so much River to cover."

"Yes, I'm sure," she said, focusing another hard stare on me. "Fortunately, you don't have to worry about it, darling."

"Why's that, Mom?"

"Because it's none of your business," she said without emotion. "Am I making myself clear?"

"Sure, sure."

Chapter 8

After dinner, Josie and I headed to the lounge to have dessert and coffee. Chef Claire, her work in the kitchen done for the evening, joined us and we relaxed in front of the roaring fire.

"How did you like the stew?" Chef Claire said, then sipped her wine.

"It was fantastic," Josie said. "How did you get the beef so tender?"

"I gave it a two-day bath in the walk-in."

"That would do the trick," Josie said. "I usually start to wrinkle after an hour."

Chief Abrams approached and sat down next to Chef Claire.

"Great meal, Chef Claire," he said, then glanced at Millie behind the bar and made a circle gesture with his finger indicating another round of drinks for the table.

"How's my mom doing?"

"She's in a pretty good mood," the Chief said. "I kept waiting for the explosion, but she's remarkably calm."

"Maybe she's mellowing with age," Josie said.

"Or on new meds," I said, then flinched when I saw two people standing at the entrance to the lounge. "Well, look who's here."

I waved until I caught their eye and they both approached.

"Look sharp, Chef Claire," Josie deadpanned.

"Don't start," she said, then sat up straight in her chair and beamed at them.

"Hi, Betty," Josie said. "Agent Tompkins. It's so nice to see you. You look great. Doesn't he look great, Chef Claire?"

"Shut it."

"Welcome," I said, gesturing at an empty couch. "Please, join us."

They shook hands with all of us then sat down.

"It's so nice to be back," Betty Smithsonian said, glancing around. "Are we too late to get dinner?"

"No, you're fine," Chef Claire said. "Let me grab you a couple of menus."

"Have the special," I said.

"Definitely," Josie said, nodding.

"Okay," Betty said. "Two specials it is. Can we eat here in the lounge?"

"Absolutely," Chef Claire said, then headed to the bar to put the order in. Moments later, she sat back down and snuck a few furtive glances at Agent Tompkins. "So, is this a social trip or are you guys working?"

"A bit of both," Agent Tompkins said, flashing Chef Claire a smile. "I've been in Ottawa the past couple of days, and Betty and I decided to drive down tonight instead of in the morning."

"Nice," Chef Claire said, nodding. "How long are you in town?"

"Just a day or two," Betty said. "Maybe longer if we need it. So, how was the rest of your time in Italy?"

"It was great," Chef Claire said. "How was your trip to California with Lance?"

"Oh, Lance," she said, then laughed and shook her head. "It was okay."

"Lance?" the Chief said, glancing around.

"He's a surfer dude who was at cooking school with us in Lake Garda," Chef Claire said, then glanced at Betty. "Can I tell them the rest of it?"

"Sure," Betty said.

"It turned out Lance works for the CIA," Chef Claire said. "He and Betty ended up capturing one of the world's most wanted arms dealers."

"With your help," Betty said.

"So, did you two end up hooking up?" Josie said with a grin. "Based on what we saw at the villa, I thought I was going to have to turn the hose on you."

"No," Betty said, then laughed. "Chalk that up to our excitement of capturing Inspector Pyscho. It was quite an adrenaline rush."

"But it wore off?" Josie said.

"It certainly did," Betty said. "Before we even got on the plane. But he did give me a surfing lesson."

"How did you do?" Chef Claire said.

"Let's just say I tried to surf once and leave it at that. It's way too hard for me."

"I take it you guys are here to do some work on the smuggling ring?" the Chief said.

"We're going to try," Agent Tompkins said. "But we seem to have stalled for the moment."

"How so?" the Chief said.

Agent Tompkins glanced around at us. Apparently comfortable with the audience, he continued.

"We thought we had figured out some things," he said. "And three days ago, we raided an oceangoing vessel that docked in Montreal. We were sure there were a bunch of people onboard being smuggled in. But we came up empty."

"Maybe the smugglers got tipped off," I said.

"It's certainly a possibility," Agent Tompkins said. "But it's more likely they're switching their process around so we can't pick up a pattern."

"Or maybe you've got a leak," I said.

"Oh, I sure hope not," Betty said, glancing at Agent Tompkins.

"That's all we need," he said. "So, we thought we'd head down here and kick the bushes to see if anything jumps out."

"We might be able to help you," the Chief said. "Suzy and I had an interesting encounter today."

The Chief spent a few minutes outlining the day's events then sat back and waited for questions.

"They panicked when they thought the Fish and Wildlife agent was a cop?" Agent Tompkins said.

"Yeah," the Chief said. "And then they chased her boat down and shot her. But she's going to be okay."

"That's what we call a good lead," Betty said.

"It certainly is," Agent Tompkins said. "Any idea where they might have gone?"

"Not a clue," the Chief said, shaking his head. "It's a big River."

"The camp must be close to where they're bringing people across," Agent Tompkins said.

"That's a logical assumption," the Chief said. "It narrows the search area, but that's about it."

"We need to find these guys," Betty said.

"You got any idea how?" Agent Tompkins said.

"Not a clue," Betty said. "Isn't that why they pay you the big bucks?"

"I thought I'd delegate that one to you," Agent Tompkins said.

"Nice try," Betty said.

"Find the dog," I said.

"What?" Betty said.

"Find the dog and you find them," I said. "At least you'll find Coke Bottle."

"Coke Bottle?" Betty said, frowning.

"That's what we call Walter," I said. "You'll understand as soon as you see him."

"How do you suggest we find the dog?" Agent Tompkins said.

"Walter's not a dog person by any stretch of the imagination," I said. "There's a chance he's had the Mastiff since it was a puppy. But it's more likely he stole the dog. He knows how valuable the Tibetans are."

"How does he know that?" Betty said.

"We had a run-in with him a while back when he was trying to steal dog semen," I said. "From a Tibetan Mastiff."

"Hey, I'm trying to eat my dessert," Josie said, frowning at me.

"Sorry," I said, then focused on the FBI agents. "When it comes to morals, Coke Bottle is pretty much bankrupt. But he loves money."

"You want to buy the dog from him?" Betty said, obviously puzzled about where I was going.

"No," I said, shaking my head. "We offer a reward for the safe return of the dog."

"Reward money?" Agent Tompkins said, perking up. "Interesting."

"A lot of reward money," I said, my neurons firing. "Something like a hundred grand. No questions asked."

"That's a lot," Betty said.

"It's not like you're going to have to pay it," I said. "But you need to make the number big enough to get his attention. Even if he's had the dog since it was a puppy, there's no way Walter wouldn't sell it for a reward that size."

"How do we get his attention?" Betty said.

"My mother knows the owner of every radio and television station and newspaper within a hundred miles. We'll just saturate the media with it. It might take a day or two, but eventually, Walter will get wind of it."

"We'll need a picture of the dog," Agent Tompkins said.

"Not a problem," I said. "We'll just find a photo of a Tibetan that looks like his."

"You know what the dog looks like?" Betty said.

"Yeah, I could probably ballpark it."

Chief Abrams laughed and almost spilled his coffee.

"It's not bad," Agent Tompkins said, nodding. "Yeah, I like it. What do you think, Betty?"

"It's better than anything else we've got," she said. "Which is nothing. I think it's worth a shot."

"We'll need a burner phone," Agent Tompkins said.

"Yeah," Betty said, nodding. "I can handle that one."

"Good," he said. "Okay, first thing in the morning we'll work up an ad. Do you think your mother will be willing to help out?"

"Of course," I said, then looked at Chief Abrams. "But you're going to have to be the one who asks her."

"Coward," the Chief said, grinning at me. "Sure, no problem. I'll ask her before I leave tonight."

"Thanks," I said. "Which one of you is going to play the role of the owner?"

The FBI agents looked at each other. Eventually, Agent Tompkins spoke.

"Actually, it might be better if neither one of us was directly involved in the transaction. I'd like to keep both of us out of sight until we're ready to arrest the guy."

"I guess that makes sense," the Chief said. "Will you guys be bringing in backup?"

"For a dog?" Agent Tompkins said. "I'd be the laughingstock of the Bureau, Chief. No, if you're willing to help out, I'm sure the three of us can handle...Coke Bottle."

"I'm not worried about Coke Bottle," the Chief said. "I'm more concerned about the dog."

"Absolutely. You better bring a tranquilizer gun," I said. "Wilbur's a beast."

"Wilbur? That's the dog's name?" Betty said.

"Yeah," I said. "Great name, huh? And he's a magnificent animal."

"Where should we do the pickup?" Betty said.

"I suggest someplace on the River near town," I said. "That way, you're forcing him to come by boat. And after you arrest him, just seize the boat. I bet Walter will come alone. And if he and his partner only have the one boat, as soon as Walter gives you the location of where he's staying, his partner should be easy to find."

"If he's willing to talk," Betty said.

"Oh, he'll talk," I said. "As long as the right person is asking the questions."

"Do you have somebody in mind?" Agent Tompkins said.

"I do."

"Who?" Betty said.

"Him," I said, pointing at Rooster who was sitting at the bar chatting with Millie.

"Who's he?" Agent Tompkins said.

"Rooster. He's Coke Bottle's cousin. And very persuasive when he wants to be."

"You think he'd be willing to set his own cousin up?" Betty said.

"Yeah, I like our chances."

"You are an evil genius," the Chief said, grinning at me.

"Thanks, Chief. That's the sweetest thing I've heard all day."

Chapter 9

I climbed out of the driver seat and headed for the back of the van. We'd bought it recently for the Inn to use for pickup and delivery of dogs either in the process of being rescued or dropped off at their new homes. If things went according to plan tonight, the van would definitely come in handy. I grabbed a duffel bag and rummaged around until I found the item I was looking for then climbed back in.

"What the heck is that thing?" Josie said, glancing over from the passenger seat.

"This is a parabolic microphone," I said, grinning at her before attaching the device to the driver side mirror. "Sweet, huh?"

"Where the heck did you get it?" Josie said, leaning over to examine the microphone.

"Amazon. Where else?" I said with a shrug. "Best two hundred bucks I've ever spent. It's good for up to a hundred yards."

I grabbed my binoculars and looked through the windshield at the dock bathed in light about a hundred feet away. Rooster was standing by himself and leaning against the railing.

"Perfect," I said, then handed Josie one of the wireless earpieces that worked with the microphone.

"Who does this place belong to?" Josie said as she inserted the earpiece.

"The Taylors," I said. "Harold and Mimi."

"I know the Taylors," Josie said, nodding. "Black lab and a Springer spaniel, right?"

"That's them. They're in Florida for the winter. Chief called them today and asked if we could use their dock."

"I take it they agreed."

"As soon as the Chief mentioned he was trying to get his hands on Coke Bottle, they were all over the idea. Apparently, they've had a few run-ins with Walter in the past."

"That guy gets around," Josie said, reaching for her binoculars. "Where are the Feds hiding?"

"Agent Tompkins said he was going to be in the pines off to our left. Betty's in the boathouse. As soon as Coke Bottle gets here, she's going to get into her boat and head for the dock."

"Where's the Chief?"

"In the boathouse, too. He'll walk over to the dock when the time is right."

"It sounds like we've got the guy surrounded," Josie said.

"Yeah, he's not going anywhere," I said, taking another look through the binoculars.

"This reminds me of when I was a kid," Josie said.

"Really?" I said, lowering the binoculars and glancing over at her. "Oh, do tell. I've gotta hear this."

"We lived across the street from my grandparents," Josie said, staring off as the memory took hold. "And they and my mom were big fans of the show, ER."

"Great show," I said, nodding.

"But my mom thought I was too young to watch it, so she always sent me upstairs to my room when it came on."

"Harsh."

"Exactly," she said. "I didn't think it was fair since I had a major crush on Clooney."

"Me too."

"It drove me nuts," she said, then laughed. "My mom's a bit hard of hearing, and the volume was always loud. So, I had no problem hearing the show from my bedroom. Then one night I realized that with a little assistance, I could also watch it."

"This oughta be good," I said, grinning at her.

"I got myself a pair of binoculars and was able to see my grandparents' TV through their front window. It worked like a charm."

"Did you get away with it?"

"I did. Until one night at the dinner table, they were discussing the latest episode, and I joined the conversation," Josie said, shaking her head. "Not the smartest thing I ever did."

"You spied on your grandparents?"

"I wasn't spying. I was watching television."

"Tomato, tomahto."

"Of all people, I would think you'd appreciate my cunning."

"Yeah, it's not bad," I said, nodding.

"Thanks."

"Hey, I forgot to mention it. I'm going fishing with the Chief and Freddie in the morning. You want to join us?"

"I would," Josie said. "But I'm booked solid. Three annual exams and a spaying before lunch."

"That's too bad," I said. "If the weather turns like they're predicting, it might be the last time we get out."

"Lights," Josie said, nodding out at the water as she raised her binoculars.

"Right on time," I said, peering through the glasses.

"My goodness, that's a big dog," Josie said.

"Did you bring the tranquilizer gun?"

"I did. And I'm pretty sure I'm going to have to use it. Geez, what a beast."

"He's gorgeous, isn't he? He'll be okay, right?"

"With getting a sedative?" Josie said, glancing over. "He'll be fine. From the looks of him, he could survive nuclear winter."

"Just don't hurt him."

"Relax. I'll give him just enough to make sure he doesn't bite my face off."

We watched the boat slowly approach the dock and come to a stop. Coke Bottle climbed out and tied the boat off. I turned the volume of the microphone up then focused the binoculars on Rooster's cousin who was tentatively making his way down the dock.

"Stay," he said, glancing back at the Tibetan who was pacing back and forth in the boat. "For once, why don't you just do as you're told?"

The dog growled his displeasure but stayed put.

"I see his eyesight hasn't improved," Josie said as she watched Coke Bottle take baby steps along the dock.

"Hello?" Coke Bottle said, coming to a stop halfway down the dock. "Is anybody here?"

Rooster cleared his throat and his cousin turned his head toward what, for him, had to be a blurred figure.

"You got my money?" Coke Bottle said, taking a few more steps closer. Hearing no response, he walked further before stopping again. "I said, have you got my money?"

Rooster cleared his throat again then coughed.

"You don't say much, do you?" Coke Bottle said, slowly removing a pistol from his coat.

Through the binoculars I could easily see the effort he was making to get a good look at the man who was now about twenty feet away. Rooster began slowly walking toward his cousin. When he was a few feet away, Coke Bottle's mouth dropped in recognition.

"Uh-oh," he whispered.

"Indeed," Rooster said, then thrust his leg forward and kicked the pistol out of his cousin's hand. The gun bounced off the dock and landed in the water with a splash. "Hello, Walter."

"Rooster."

"Indeed," Rooster repeated.

"Long time no see, huh?" Coke Bottle said, glancing around for potential escape routes. "What are you doing here?"

"I'm here to beat the crap out of you."

"There's no need to do that, Rooster," he said, taking a step backward. "We're family, right?"

"You'll have to do better than that," Rooster said, taking a step forward. "Give me another reason."

"Uh, let's see…"

"Time's up," Rooster said, then fired a punch that knocked Coke Bottle off his feet.

The Tibetan barked loudly as he paced back and forth but remained in the boat.

"Nice shot," Josie said, continuing to watch the action through her binoculars.

"Yeah, that had to hurt," I said, nodding. "I can't believe how good he moves for an old guy."

"I can't believe he's wearing shorts and work boots with no socks."

We both stifled laughs and focused on the dock.

Rooster looked at the dog. Satisfied it was staying put for the moment, he knelt down and hammered Coke Bottle three more times. His cousin spat blood and reached around the immediate vicinity for his glasses. Rooster grabbed the glasses and handed them to his cousin who shakily put them back on.

"Sit up," Rooster said.

Coke Bottle complied and managed to get upright with his legs splayed.

"I thought I made myself perfectly clear, Walter."

"I'm sittin' up, aren't I?" Coke Bottle said, confused.

"Not about that, you idiot. I was referring to our last conversation in Pennsylvania. You remember that, don't you, Walter?"

"Hard to forget that one, Rooster. I was coughing up blood for three days."

"What part of banished don't you understand?"

"Huh?" Coke Bottle said, squinting up at him.

"It means to *stay away*, Walter. What the hell are you doing back in town?"

"Uh…vacation?"

"I probably would have gone with visiting for Thanksgiving," Rooster said, then fired another punch that knocked his cousin flat on his back. "But it's your lie, so who am I to judge? Sit up. I repeat, what are you doing here?"

"The ad said no questions asked," Coke Bottle said, adjusting his glasses that were bent and perched precariously on the tip of his nose.

"Advertisers, huh? I guess you can't believe anything you read these days. Where did you get the dog?"

"Does it matter?"

"I'm sure it does to the person you stole him from," Rooster said. "It was the breeder in Pennsylvania, wasn't it?"

Coke Bottle stared off into space before eventually nodding.

"Yeah, that's where I got him."

"When did you steal him?"

"About a month ago," Coke Bottle said. "But it seems like a year. That dog is a lot of work."

"I imagine he's hard to control. You know, since the dog is so much smarter than you are."

"You don't need to be mean, Rooster," Coke Bottle whispered.

"Oh, I'm just getting started," Rooster said, then fired another vicious punch. "Sit up."

"I might be a slow learner, but I'm not a total idiot. I think I'll stay right here."

"Either sit up or you're going to get my boot in the ribs," Rooster said, taking a step closer.

"Okay. Hang on. This is gonna take me a minute," he said, slowly pushing himself upright with both arms.

"Where's your partner?" Rooster said.

"Partner?"

"You playing dumb, Walter, or do you need the definition?"

"I don't have a clue what you're talking about."

"Last time I'm going to ask you, Walter. Where's the guy who helped you tie Chief Abrams to the chair?"

"Oh, you heard about that?"

"Small town," Rooster said. "Where is he?"

Coke Bottle sat quietly and took several deep breaths before making eye contact.

"He's over at Willander."

"Willander?" Rooster said, surprised. "You went to my island?"

"Yeah," Coke Bottle said. "It seemed like a good idea at the time. You've got the place closed up for the winter. And it's remote. We ain't seen a single boat go by since we got there."

"Tell me about this smuggling ring you're involved in," Rooster said.

"What smuggling ring?"

"You want another one?" Rooster said, drawing his arm back.

"Do what you need to do, Rooster. But I ain't saying a word about that." Then he cocked his head, confused. "Not that I know anything about any smuggling."

Rooster fired another punch and Coke Bottle fell back again, his legs rising before landing on the dock with a loud thud.

"Sit up."

"I'm gonna need some help," Coke Bottle eventually managed to get out.

Rooster pulled him upright by his coat and continued to stand over him.

"Some guard dog you are," Coke Bottle said, glancing at the boat.

84

"He's obviously a good judge of character," Rooster said, looking at the dog who continued to pace the boat closely watching the proceedings. Then he took a step back and said loudly, "Okay, I'm done here."

"Who are you talking to?"

"You'll see," Rooster said, massaging his hands.

"Does this mean I'm not getting my money?"

"Take a wild guess," Rooster said, shaking his head.

He looked down the dock where Agent Tompkins and the Chief were converging. They casually strolled down the dock and came to a stop next to Rooster.

"I'm glad you stopped when you did," Agent Tompkins said. "I thought you were going to kill him for a minute there."

"Nah," Rooster said. "It just takes a few extra shots to get through his cement head. Doesn't it, Walter?"

"Go to hell, Rooster," he said, wiping his glasses with a sleeve. "Hey, Chief."

"Walter," Chief Abrams said as he rocked back and forth on his heels.

"Sorry about the other day. I panicked when I saw you heading for the cabin."

"Yes, I noticed," the Chief said.

"How the heck did you get loose?" Coke Bottle said, frowning. "I tied you up myself."

"Divine intervention, I guess."

"Huh?"

"Never mind."

"Who's this guy?" Coke Bottle said, nodding at Agent Tompkins.

"Oh, I'm sorry, Walter," Rooster said, then laughed. "How rude of me. I'd like you to meet Agent Tompkins from the FBI."

"FBI? Crap."

"Indeed," Rooster said. "He's all yours, Agent Tompkins."

"Thanks, Rooster," Agent Tompkins said, then fixed a cocky grin on Rooster's cousin who was bleeding profusely all over the dock. "It's nice to meet you, Walter."

"Yeah, likewise," Coke Bottle said, unable to make eye contact.

"Hang on a sec," Agent Tompkins said to no one in particular. "Ladies, we're going to take Walter out of here. Please hold your position until we get him in the car. Then we'll deal with the dog. How do you want to handle it from here, Chief?"

"I've got a nice cell all ready for Walter," the Chief said. "I thought you and I would get him settled in for the night. Rooster, would you mind sticking around to help with the dog?"

"No problem," Rooster said, then gave his cousin a swift kick in the ribs. "It'll be nice dealing with a higher lifeform."

Walter groaned loudly then looked back and forth at the two cops.

"Are you just going to stand there and let him do that to me?"

"I gotta say, Walter," the Chief said. "I was thinking about doing the same thing."

"But you didn't because you're a cop, right?" Walter said, struggling to get the words out.

"No, because Rooster offered to do it for me."

Betty drove the boat out of the boathouse and slowly approached the dock. She turned the engine off, and the boat gently rocked in the shallow water.

"I guess you didn't need me," she said, glancing around. "Where's the island he mentioned?"

"It's pretty easy to find," Rooster said. "You just head about three miles out toward Rockport on the Canadian side. As soon as you see the town in front of you, make a right, and you'll run straight into Willander about a mile downriver. It's the one with a big log cabin house."

"How long a trip is it?" Betty said.

"At cruising speed, about fifteen, twenty minutes," Rooster said.

"Okay, thanks, Rooster," Betty said, then glanced at Agent Tompkins. "I think we should probably wait until morning. I really don't want to be out on the River at this time of night."

"Makes sense," Agent Tompkins said, nodding in agreement. Then he looked at Rooster. "Are there any boats at your island?"

"No, I bring them all back to my marina during the winter," Rooster said. "As long as the idiots don't have another boat, his partner isn't going anywhere." Rooster nudged his cousin with his boot. "You got a second boat over there?"

"No," Coke Bottle said, shaking his head.

"Are you lying to me, Walter?" Rooster said, drawing his leg back.

"No, I ain't lyin'," Walter said, flinching. "That's the only boat we got."

"I think I believe him," Agent Tompkins said. "But if you're lying, it's only going to make things worse for you."

"I ain't lyin'," Coke Bottle said.

"Okay," Agent Tompkins said. "Let's get him locked up. We'll collect him tomorrow after we pick up his partner. Is that all right with you, Chief?"

"Not a problem," Chief Abrams said. "I've got my deputy coming in to keep an eye on things tonight and tomorrow morning."

"You're not going to be there?" Agent Tompkins said.

"I'll be around, but I'm going fishing first thing in the morning for a couple of hours. Don't worry. George is good at his job. Walter's not going anywhere."

"I'll take the boat back," Betty said. "Should I meet you at the police station?"

"No, I think the Chief and I will be able to handle it," Agent Tompkins said. "Tell you what. Why don't we meet at C's later?"

"Sounds good," Betty said, starting the engine. "Will an hour be enough time?"

"Yeah, that should be plenty," Agent Tompkins said. "See you there."

"Have fun," Betty said, then accelerated away from the dock.

"Let's get him to his feet," Chief Abrams said.

All three men lifted Coke Bottle to his feet. He wobbled back and forth until Rooster and Chief Abrams both grabbed an arm and slowly escorted him down the dock.

"Just one more question, Walter," Agent Tompkins said.

"What now?"

"What's your partner's name?"

Walter remained silent until he winced when Rooster squeezed his arm.

"Ow," Coke Bottle said, glaring at his cousin. "His name is Roger. Roger Smith."

"Roger Smith?" Agent Tompkins said, surprised. "Well, how about that?"

"You know the guy?" Chief Abrams said.

"Nothing gets past him, right?" I said to Josie.

"Shut it," she said, stifling a laugh. "I want to hear this."

"Oh, yeah," Agent Tompkins said. "I know Roger."

Chapter 10

"Okay, we're up," I said, climbing out of the van and heading for the back. I opened the hatch and grabbed a dog lead and a blanket. "Don't forget the tranquilizer gun."

"Not a chance," Josie said, holding it up for me to see. "Let's get this done. I'm getting hungry."

We strolled down to the dock and were met by Rooster who continued to massage his hands.

"You were pretty rough on him," I said, gently examining the back of his right hand.

"He's just lucky the cops were around," Rooster said, staring at the boat where the Tibetan continued to pace from bow to stern and back. "Let's go get the dog and then I'm going to let you guys buy me dinner."

We laughed and followed him down the dock. When we reached the boat, the dog seemed to recognize me and put its front paws up on the side of the boat and emitted his trademark guttural growl.

"Geez," Josie said, shaking her head. "He's even bigger than I expected. I wonder what he eats."

"Probably anything he wants to," I said. "Hi, Wilbur. Who's the good dog?"

The dog began barking furiously when he heard my voice and pawed the top rail of the boat. Judging by the look on his face, he was apparently trying to decide if he could make the jump from the boat to the dock and grab me by the throat without falling in the water.

"You usually don't have this effect on dogs," Josie said with a grin.

"Yeah, I must be losing my touch," I said, keeping a close eye on the dog. "You think we should try to get him without using the sedative?"

"Not a chance," Josie and Rooster said in unison.

"Okay," I said. "But be careful. How much are you going to use?"

"A lot," Josie said, then focused on the Tibetan. "I'm sorry, Wilbur. Try not to take this personally."

Josie extended her arm and fired into the Tibetan's upper front leg. The dog snarled and did his best to get his mouth on the protruding dart. The dog continued to growl as it resumed pacing the boat with a small limp.

"I feel terrible," I said, studying the dog's movements.

"He'll be fine," Josie said. "And we'll keep a close eye on him tonight while he's napping."

"How long does it take for that stuff to take effect?" Rooster said.

"He'll start slowing down in a few minutes," Josie said. "And he should be sleeping like a baby in a half-hour, forty-five minutes top."

"Okay, then I guess we wait," Rooster said, sitting down on the dock. "Nice night."

"I can't believe you aren't freezing your butt off," Josie said, sitting down next to him and pulling a bag of bite-sized from her coat pocket. She offered the bag to Rooster who waved them off. I grabbed a small handful and leaned against the railing. "What do you think the cops are going to do to your cousin?"

"Interrogate the crap out of him," Rooster said. "And they'll decide what to do next based on what he tells them."

"It sounded like he's definitely involved in the smuggling ring," I said, popping one of the bite-sized into my mouth.

"Yeah, I'm sure he is," Rooster said. "If there's criminal activity going on within a hundred miles, Walter's usually up to his neck in it."

"It has to be a pretty lucrative operation," Josie said, sliding the bag back into her pocket. "A hundred grand a pop."

"Yeah, especially if you're bringing people in by the dozen," I said. "Since he was using Jackson's camp and then your place over on Willander, I'm wondering if they're dropping the people off on the Canadian side near Rockport."

"It makes sense," Rooster said. "Not a lot of people around. Lots of remote places to make the drop-offs and pick-ups."

"And then it's only a short boat ride," I said. "There must be a hundred spots they could use to land on the U.S. side."

"At least," Rooster said, glancing at the boat. "He's starting to settle down."

"Yeah, it won't be long," Josie said, popping her final bite-sized. "I hit him pretty good."

"Vicious animal," Rooster said.

"He's just scared," I said, staring at the dog.

"Scared?" Rooster said, shaking his head. "If that's scared, I don't want to be around when he's angry."

"He's out of his element," I said. "And has been for the past month. I'm sure he misses his papa."

"You still got that breeder's number?" Rooster said.

"Yeah, it's in my office somewhere," I said. "I'll give him a call as soon as we get Wilbur settled into his condo."

We sat chatting quietly about nothing for the next half-hour waiting for the dog to nod off. When we heard the massive beast begin snoring softly, Josie got to her feet and slowly approached the boat.

"Okay, he's out," she said. "How do you want to do this?"

"Let's pull the boat to the other end of the dock and get the bow on shore," Rooster said, standing up. "Stretch the blanket out on the dock. I'll lift him out."

"By yourself?" I said.

"Sure," Rooster said, untying the bowline.

I glanced at Josie who shrugged back. We pulled the boat down the dock then heard the bow gently scrape against the rocks on shore. Rooster left the dock and headed for the boat. He peered over the edge of the bow and studied the dog's movements. Or lack thereof. Satisfied the dog was sound asleep, he climbed into the boat then lifted the dog in both arms. He gently placed the dog on the blanket then climbed out and rejoined us on the dock.

"How did you do that?" I said, marveling at his strength and the ease at which he'd handled the dog.

"I'm old, not decrepit," he said, grinning at me.

"Still, he has to weigh close to two hundred pounds," Josie said.

"Chalk it up to clean living," he said, kneeling down and wrapping the blanket around the snoring dog. He again picked the Tibetan up and began walking toward our van. "He is a bruiser. I'll give him that."

Josie trotted ahead to open the side door of the van. I did my best lumber and eventually met her at the van. Josie lowered the back seat then got out of the way. Rooster gently placed the dog on the seat then climbed in next to the Tibetan.

"Okay," he said. "Just in case that stuff wears off in a hurry, let's get him to the Inn."

"He'll be out for a while," Josie said, climbing in the passenger seat.

I got in and started the van. Five minutes later, we were at the Inn. Sammy and Jill met us at the front door.

"You guys got the condo ready?" I said, heading into the registration area.

"Yeah, it's all set," Sammy said. "You said you were bringing in a big dog, so we went with the large condo at the end of the south wall."

"Good call," Josie said, holding the door open for Rooster who had the dog in his arms.

"Holy crap," Jill said, taking a step back when she got her first look at the Tibetan. "Are you sure that's a dog?"

"Big, huh?" I said, laughing.

Rooster headed for the back of the Inn followed closely by Sammy.

"Make sure the condo lock is secure, Sammy," Josie said.

"No worries there," Sammy said.

"Would you guys mind sticking around for a while?" Josie said to Jill.

"Not at all," Jill said. "Chef Claire dropped some dinner off for us before she went to the restaurant. We'll just eat here."

"Thanks," Josie said. "He should be out for at least a couple hours if not longer. Just keep a close eye on him and if he comes to, or seems to be having any trouble breathing, give me a call. I'll be at C's. But I'll be back to relieve you in a couple of hours."

"You got it," Jill said, heading off to the condo area.

Josie and I headed for my office, and I rummaged through my collection of business cards until I found the one I was looking for. I made the call and waited.

"Highland Hills Breeders. This is Roger."

"Hi, Mr. Highland. I'm not sure if you remember me, but my name is Suzy Chandler."

"Chandler? Rings a bell. Sure, I remember. You were here a while back looking for a guy you thought was trying to steal my dog."

"That's me," I said.

"You were here with your friend, Chicken, right?"

"Rooster."

"Right. Sorry. How can I help you?"

"One of your Tibetans went missing about a month ago."

"How the heck did you know that?" he said, puzzled at first. "Did you see one of my ads offering a reward?"

"No," I said. "But we have him."

"You've got Wilbur?"

"We do," I said. "He's safe and sound. At the moment, he's sleeping peacefully in one of our dog condos."

"Now I remember. You run some sort of dog hotel."

"We do. Wilbur's in good hands."

"That's the best news I've had in a long time, Ms. Chandler," he said softly. "But the timing could be better."

"Why's that?"

"I'm about to head to the airport. I'm spending Thanksgiving with my daughter in Hawaii. But I suppose I could figure out a way to get him picked up."

"He'll be fine with us until you get back, Mr. Highland."

"Are you sure?"

"Positive."

"If I remember, you said you lived in Upstate New York in the Thousand Islands."

"Yes. In Clay Bay."

"I take Route 81 all the way until I hit the bridge to Canada, right?"

"Yeah, you can't miss it."

"It's about five or six hours?" he said.

"Yeah, weather permitting," I said. "When would you like to pick him up?"

"I'll be on the road as soon as I land on Friday," he said. "It'll probably be late by the time I get there."

"We'll be here," I said. "Just give me a call when you get close, and I'll give you directions to our place."

"I'll do that," he said. "And I'll bring the reward money with me."

"No, don't worry about that," I said. "Keep it. You can use it to buy him food."

Roger Highland laughed into the phone.

"I can't thank you enough," he said. "I've been worried sick about him. Are you sure he's okay?"

"He's fine," I said, then glanced at Josie who nodded for me to continue. "But I should tell you we had to use a tranquilizer gun on him tonight."

"I see," he whispered. "I wish you hadn't had to do that."

"Me too," I said. "But there was no way we could control him without it."

"Yeah, I get it," he said. "I imagine he's been out of sorts since he was stolen."

"My business partner is a vet, and she handled the dosage," I said. "I assure you he's going to be fine."

"Okay," he said. "Did you catch the guy who stole him?"

"We did. And he's already in jail."

"Good," he said. "Hey, it didn't happen to be the same guy as the last time?"

"As a matter of fact, it was."

"I'd sure like to have a little chat with him when I get there."

"I don't think that's going to be possible," I said. "I imagine the FBI is going to call dibs."

"FBI, huh? I assume he was doing other things besides stealing dogs."

"That's what it looks like," I said. "But if it makes you feel any better, the guy did get roughed up a bit tonight."

Josie snorted and I motioned for her to be quiet.

"Good. Okay, I'll let you go. Thanks again. I'll be in touch."

"Goodnight, Mr. Highland. Have a great time in Hawaii."

"Thanks," he said. "I really appreciate your help."

I slid the phone into my pocket.

"Roughed up a bit?" Josie said with a grin.

"Yeah, it sounded nicer than felony assault," I said, getting out of my chair. "You ready to eat?"

"Rhetorical, right?"

We made the short drive to C's and entered through the kitchen door. Chef Claire was sitting at the chef's table in the back and chatting with a couple of her staff.

"Hey, how did it go?" Chef Claire said, getting to her feet.

"Not bad at all," I said. "Coke Bottle's in custody and bleeding profusely from several spots."

"Good. And the dog?"

"Sleeping it off at the Inn," Josie said. "Did you eat yet?"

"No, I was waiting for you guys," she said, removing her chef's hat and coat. She glanced at her staff. "I assume you can take it from here?"

"Yeah, I think we got it, Chef Claire," Charlie, her sous chef, said, then turned to Josie and me. "I recommend the special. It's a pork chop in a mushroom cream sauce over spinach fettuccine."

"Perfect," Josie said. "With the house salad if you don't mind."

"Make that two," I said.

"Three," Chef Claire said. "We'll eat in the lounge, Charlie."

We followed her out of the kitchen and stopped at the bar to say hi to Millie. I glanced around the empty lounge then back at Millie.

"Slow night, huh?"

"We had a bit of a rush earlier, but that's it," Millie said, pouring wine for Josie and Chef Claire. She handed me a glass of club soda with lime.

"Have you seen Chief Abrams?" I said between sips.

"No, but he called a few minutes ago to make sure the kitchen was still open."

"Thanks," I said, heading for one of the couches in front of the fire.

We sat down and felt the warmth surround us. I removed my jacket and adjusted the sweatshirt I was wearing underneath it. I took a few more sips then heard the front door open. Betty Smithsonian entered and waved as she approached.

"Did you stop by the police station?" I said.

"No, after I took the boat back, I swung by the hotel to take a quick shower. I got a chill out there tonight."

"The Chief just called and said he and Agent Tompkins are on their way."

"Great," she said. "I'm starving. How are you, Chef Claire?"

"Couldn't be better. I hear you arrested Coke Bottle tonight. Well done."

"Yeah," she said, shaking her head. "That was quite a beating Rooster gave him. I'm sure he bled all over Chief Abram's car."

"Good," Chef Claire said. "The beating, not the blood in the car."

"You seem to have a rather strong animosity toward Walter," Betty said.

"He stole my Goldens," Chef Claire said with a shrug.

"So, what's the plan for tomorrow?" I said, then drained the last of my club soda.

"Agent Tompkins and I will head to Rooster's island and arrest Roger Smith," she said, accepting the glass of wine Millie was holding out. "Thanks, Millie. I just hope we don't have to shoot it out with him."

"Is he some sort of marksman?" Josie said.

"I don't think so," Betty said. "But I hate getting into shootouts first thing in the morning. Especially if I haven't had my coffee."

We all laughed then glanced at the door when Chief Abrams and Agent Tompkins entered.

"How did it go?" Betty said to her colleague.

"No problems at all," Agent Tompkins said as he sat down and beamed at Chef Claire. "Walter is resting comfortably. Or at least as comfortable as you can be after what he went through.

And Chief Abram's deputy is on his way to the station to keep an eye on him."

"We'll pick him up after we grab Roger?" Betty said.

"Yeah. We'll take both of them to the field office in Buffalo," Agent Tompkins said. "Based on what they give us, we'll figure out our next steps."

"Sounds like a plan," Betty said, nodding.

"Who's Roger Smith?" I said.

"He's a notorious counterfeiter who dropped off the radar a couple years ago," Agent Tompkins said. "It's getting a lot harder to counterfeit currency, so my guess is he's moved into documents."

"You think he's the one who's handling the new identities of the people they're smuggling in?" I said.

"Yeah, I'm almost positive," he said. "We'll confirm it in the morning."

"But for the rest of the evening, we relax," Betty said.

"I'll drink to that," Agent Tompkins said, stifling a yawn. Then he glanced at the Chief. "I can't believe you're going fishing in the morning. It's going to be freezing out there."

"You'll be out there, too," Chief Abrams said.

"Yeah, but I have to be," Agent Tompkins said with a grin. "What's your excuse?"

Chapter 11

Freddie watched despondently as Chief Abrams landed his fourth Northern Pike in the past hour. The Chief held the fish to his chest, carefully removed the hook then leaned over the side of the boat and slid it back into the water. It disappeared with a flick of its tail. He set his pole down and grabbed a thermos then topped off our mugs of hot chocolate.

"Relax, Freddie," the Chief said, laughing when he caught the look on the medical examiner's face. "It's just not your day."

"I should have stayed in bed," Freddie said, reeling in his line. "I think I'll take a break and enjoy the sunrise." He sat down in the stern and stretched his legs out in front of him. "How many folks are coming to Thanksgiving dinner at the restaurant?"

"The last count was two-fifty and climbing," I said, casting. "Last year, we did a little over three hundred. What have you been up to lately, Freddie? I haven't seen you around."

"I started my new hobby," he said.

"Oh, that's right," I said. "Your annual winter self-improvement project. What is it this year?"

"Origami."

"You're going to spend the winter folding paper?" Chief Abrams said, raising an eyebrow.

"I am," Freddie said, nodding. "My plan is to master the ancient Japanese art of Origami."

"Good for you," the Chief deadpanned. "Make me a new car when you get a chance. I think mine is on its last legs."

"Don't be mean," I said to the Chief.

"That's okay, Suzy," Freddie said. "I'm used to him by now. But you should see some of the stuff I'm doing with dollar bills."

"I can't wait," Chief Abrams said, leaning his pole against the side of the boat.

"No, I'm serious," Freddie said. "Rings, bowties, butterflies. I do a bunch of different things. Tonight, I'm going to try to make a dog."

"We need to find you a girlfriend, Freddie," the Chief said.

"No argument from me."

"Which breed?" I said, also putting my pole away.

"It's a bulldog," Freddie said. "I thought I'd give it to Jackson. You know, since he has one."

"Got it," I said, glancing at the Chief who continued to stare in disbelief at the medical examiner.

"Did you guys hear he found a buyer for the store?" Freddie said.

"We did," I said.

"Why the guy would want to buy a grocery store in the hinterlands is beyond me," Freddie said.

I flinched when my neurons flared but quickly recovered.

"What is it?" Chief Abrams said.

"Nothing," I said, shaking my head. "I just got a chill."

"Okay," he said, studying my expression closely.

The Chief's phone rang, and he set it down on the seat next to him.

"This is Chief Abrams."

"Good morning, Chief. You catching anything besides a cold?"

"Oh, hey, Agent Tompkins. Yeah, they've been biting good this morning. Are you at Willander Island yet?"

"Yeah, we got here a few minutes ago," the FBI agent said softly.

"Well, I don't hear any gunfire," the Chief said, then chuckled. "So, I guess it must be going well."

"No, there's was no need to shoot it out."

"He surrendered quietly?"

"Well, he's definitely been quiet," Agent Tompkins said.

"You need my help?" the Chief said.

"Actually, I was calling to get the phone number of your local medical examiner. Freddie, right?"

"Uh-oh," I whispered.

"Who's dead?" the Chief said.

"Roger Smith. Shot once in the chest and another in the head."

"How long has he been dead?" the Chief said.

"It's been awhile. That's why I need to get in touch with your guy."

"Hang on," the Chief said. "Freddie's right here."

Freddie approached and leaned down close to the phone.

"Hi, Agent Tompkins. This is Freddie."

"Hey, Freddie. Sorry to ruin your fishing, but I could use your help over here."

"Don't worry about it," Freddie said. "You're at Rooster's place on Willander?"

"We are," Agent Tompkins said. "How far away are you guys?"

"Fifteen minutes max," I said, sitting down behind the steering wheel.

"Okay, I'll see you guys when you get here," Agent Tompkins said. "Just come on up to the house. Betty and I will be in the living room."

He ended the call and Freddie handed the phone back to the Chief. They both took a seat and hunkered down for warmth as I accelerated. We didn't see a single boat as we crossed the River and headed for Rockport. When I spotted the town, I veered right and continued at high speed downriver until Willander Island came into view. I slowed as I neared the dock and Freddie hopped out and tied the boat off. Chief Abrams climbed out then extended a hand to help me onto the dock. I groaned from the effort and arched my back.

"I think this is definitely going to be my last ride of the year," I said, shaking my head. "It's just too hard getting in and out of the boat."

"You're doing fine," the Chief said, patting my hand. "In fact, you're glowing."

"It's probably windburn," I said, bouncing on my toes as I hugged myself for warmth.

"Okay, let's go check out the dead guy," the Chief said.

We headed down the dock then up the path toward a large log home. Freddie glanced around when he got his first good look at the house and whistled softly.

"Wow. What a place."

"You've never been here before?" I said.

"No. I've driven by the island before but never got a good look at the house," Freddie said. "It's amazing."

"Rooster built it about ten years ago," I said.

"When you say built it, you mean he hired some guys, right?"

"No," I said, shaking my head. "He had some help putting up the walls and roof, but he did most of it himself."

"A man of many talents," Freddie said.

"Yes, some men build massive structures," the Chief deadpanned. "Others fold paper."

"Funny, Chief," Freddie said, climbing the steps.

The Chief knocked then opened the door. We headed for the living room and found Betty and Agent Tompkins along with the body of Roger Smith. Betty was pacing but stopped when she saw us. Agent Tompkins ended his phone call then stood.

"Thanks for coming," Agent Tompkins said.

"Hi, guys," Betty said.

"Hey, Betty," I said, giving her a quick hug. "Well, at least your morning didn't start with a shootout."

"Yeah," she said, forcing a small laugh. "But that might have been preferable to looking at him. What a mess."

"Indeed," Freddie said, studying the body sprawled in front of the fireplace. "Did you check for embers in the fire?"

"I did," Agent Tompkins said. "It's just ash. The fire's been out for hours."

"Okay," Freddie said, glancing around. "I need some gloves."

"Kitchen," I said, nodding in the general direction.

"I'll be right back," Freddie said, heading off.

"He got shot at close range," the Chief said.

"Yeah," Betty said. "Impossible to miss from that close."

I glanced at the Chief who nodded, apparently thinking the same thing I was. Freddie returned pulling on a pair of rubber gloves.

"Have you seen that kitchen?" he said, glancing over his shoulder. "He's got a built-in fridge and sub-zero freezer." Freddie knelt down over the body and began to gently probe. "Cold with pretty advanced rigor."

"What's your best guess about the time of death?" Agent Tompkins said, kneeling next to Freddie.

"I'll need a few minutes," he said.

"Sure, take your time," Agent Tompkins said, standing up. "I didn't mean to rush you."

"No problem," Freddie said, now focused intensely on his work.

"I can't believe it," Betty said.

"Hey, I don't like it any more than you," Agent Tompkins said. "But we play the cards we're dealt, right?"

"This could set us back months," she said, staring out the picture window that dominated the room.

"Unless Walter starts talking," Agent Tompkins said.

"Do you really think that idiot knows how the operation works?" Betty said, glaring at her colleague.

"There's only one way to find out," Agent Tompkins said. "And he might be more willing to chat with a murder charge hanging over his head."

"Yeah, let's hope so," Betty said, then kicked at the floor with the toe of her shoe. "Damn it. I thought we'd caught the break we needed."

"Hang in there," Agent Tompkins said. "Let's not worry about it until we get a chance to talk with Walter."

"Did you find any equipment?" I said.

"Like what?" Betty said.

"You said last night the guy was a counterfeiter," I said. "Did you find anything he might be using to make fake documents?"

"We haven't had a chance yet," Agent Tompkins said, then glanced at Betty. "I guess this is as good a time as any."

"I'll check the bedrooms," she said, heading off.

"What do you think, Chief?" Agent Tompkins said.

"About Walter shooting his partner at point-blank range? Yeah, I have no problem making that work. You've met the guy. And we know he's blind as a bat."

"Yeah, but why would he do it?"

"Maybe they were fighting about money," I said.

"Or maybe Walter was getting cold feet about being involved," the Chief said. "He might have been thinking about taking the hundred grand in reward money and hitting the road."

"I don't know, Chief," I said. "Rooster had already warned him twice about staying away. Even that didn't do the trick. I don't think Walter is a cut and run kind of guy."

"Yeah, you might be right," the Chief said. "Too dumb to feel fear."

"He's definitely a box of rocks," I said. "Rooster wouldn't have to tell me more than once."

"You got that right," the Chief said.

Betty returned to the living room, now wearing gloves and holding a stack of objects in her hands.

"Computer, high-end printer, and a couple of boxes of materials," she said, holding out one of the items to Agent Tompkins. "Passports, birth certificates, New York state driver's licenses."

Agent Tompkins *snapped* on a pair of gloves and inspected the passport Betty was holding out.

"It's nice to see Roger hadn't lost his touch," Agent Tompkins said, looking through some of the other items. "This is good stuff."

"It is," Betty said. "But I didn't find anything that might tell us when the next delivery is."

"Too bad," Agent Tompkins said. "But we do have photos of everybody who's being smuggled in."

"We can get copies to all the local cops and state police," the Chief said, grabbing his phone. He began taking pictures of all the passport photos. "Maybe we'll get lucky and they'll spot one of them."

"It can't hurt," Agent Tompkins said.

"I doubt if they're going to be sticking around the area after they're dropped off," Betty said.

"Yeah, probably not," Agent Tompkins said.

"But we play the cards we're dealt, right?" Betty said with a grin.

"There you go," Agent Tompkins said, then laughed.

"Okay, here's what I know," Freddie said, getting to his feet. "My best estimate is he's been dead somewhere between

111

twelve and twenty-four hours. The rigor is definitely set in, and the body is stone cold. Since the fire's been out for quite a while, last night's cold probably sped the rigor process up a bit. And judging by the size of the wound in his chest, the shot to the head was overkill. I'll know more after I get him back to my office and do some slicing and dicing."

"Geez, Freddie," I said, scowling. "Must you?"

"Sorry," he said. "I need to get some folks out here to remove the body."

"Not a problem," Agent Tompkins said, then turned to Betty. "You mind staying here with Freddie while I head back with the Chief and start talking to Walter?"

"That's fine," Betty said. "I'll meet you at the police station later."

"Did you find either bullet?" Agent Tompkins said.

"Not yet," Freddie said. "My guess is the shooter used hollow points. They're probably still in there."

"They're the ones that mushroom on impact, right?" I said.

"That's them," Chief Abrams said.

"Lovely," I said, frowning. "Geez, Coke Bottle. What the heck is the matter with you?"

"Probably got dropped on his head when he was a kid," Betty said. "Murder one and human-trafficking. That dude is going away for a very long time."

"Works for me," Agent Tompkins said. "Okay, Chief. Are you ready to hit the road?"

"Let's do it," the Chief said.

"You think you can get Coke Bottle to talk?" I said to Agent Tompkins as we headed for the door.

"Well, if I can't, I certainly know who to call."

"Rooster would love another shot at him," the Chief said, nodding.

"I don't think I can let that happen," Agent Tompkins said. "But the *threat* of it just might be enough."

Chapter 12

George McDaniel was a man in his forties who'd left the military after getting his twenty years in. Soon after George left the service, Chief Abrams hired him as his deputy, and, over the years, he'd proven himself to be a dedicated and competent cop. When we entered the police station, he was sitting with his feet up on the desk reading a magazine. He glanced up when he heard us and gave us a small wave.

"Comfy?" the Chief said, then laughed.

"Hey, I learned from the master," George said, lowering his feet and standing up.

"Agent Tompkins," the Chief said. "This is my deputy, George McDaniel."

"Nice to meet you," Agent Tompkins said, giving the deputy a firm handshake that made him wince.

"Same here," George said. "Hey, Suzy. How are you doing?"

"I'm great, George. How's the new puppy working out?"

"He's amazing," George said, then looked at the FBI agent. "I just adopted a lab mix from Suzy." Then he turned back to me. "He's really smart. Almost housebroken already."

"Glad to hear it," I said, sitting down on the other side of the desk.

"How's our friend doing?" the Chief said, nodding in the direction of the cells located behind the office.

"Haven't heard a peep out of him," George said. "I checked in on him when I got here last night, but he was out. I imagine he's still licking his wounds. Rooster tuned him up pretty good last night."

"Okay, George," the Chief said, removing his coat. "I can take it from here. Why don't you head home and get some sleep?" The Chief patted his pockets then frowned. "Dang it. I left my keys at the house. You mind letting us in before you head out?"

"No problem, Chief," George said, heading for the door that led to the cells.

"Do you mind if I tag along?" I said.

"You're asking me for permission?" the Chief said, confused.

"Actually, I was asking him," I said, then laughed as I pointed at Agent Tompkins.

"It's fine with me," Agent Tompkins said. "But you better let me handle the questions. You know, all those pesky Bureau regulations."

"Got it," I said with a grin.

George unlocked the door and pulled it open. He stood back to let us get past, and we stepped through the door into an area where three small jail cells were located. All three of us took a look around then stared at each other.

"Uh, George," the Chief called out in a singsong voice.

"Yeah," George said.

"Could you come in here for a second, please?" the Chief said.

"Sure," George said, poking his head through the doorway. "What's up?"

"You tell me," the Chief said, gesturing with one arm.

"What the hell?" George said, glancing around the three empty cells.

"Are you kidding me?" Agent Tompkins said, glaring at the deputy.

"Where the heck did he go?" George said, bewildered. "I was sitting at the desk all night."

"Are you sure?" the Chief said, nodding for us to follow him back into the office. He sat down behind his desk and stared hard at George. "Talk to me, George."

"I swear, Chief. I was here all night," he said, then frowned. "Except for…"

"Here we go," Agent Tompkins said, shaking his head.

"Except for what, George?" the Chief said, enunciating each word slowly.

"I got a call from Jackson around one in the morning," George said, sitting down. "One of the motion detectors got tripped at the store, and the silent alarm at his house went off. I met him over there a couple of minutes later. It must have been kids or an animal because there were no signs of a break-in.

Then I headed straight back here. I couldn't have been gone more than fifteen minutes."

"Damn," the Chief whispered. "I'm so sorry, Agent Tompkins."

"Not half as sorry as I am," he said, giving George another hard stare. He exhaled loudly and rubbed his forehead. "Okay, let's talk this through. How many sets of keys are there to the front door and the cells?"

"Three," the Chief said. "We each have a set, and we keep a spare locked up."

"Did you take your keys with you when you left last night?" Agent Tompkins said to George.

"I did," George said with a firm nod. "I never leave them here."

"Did you lock the front door when you left?" the Chief said.

"Uh, I think so," George said, frowning. "Maybe."

"Great," Agent Tompkins whispered, then shook his head again. "Where's the spare set of keys?"

"In one of those filing cabinets," George said.

"Which one?" Agent Tompkins said, glancing around.

"My guess would be the one with the broken lock," I said, nodding at a filing cabinet next to the desk.

"Damn," the Chief said, leaning over to inspect the damage.

"But how the heck would anybody know they were there?" George said.

"As far as I know, we're the only two people who knew it," the Chief said. "Have you mentioned it to anybody?"

"Do I look like an idiot?" George said, his temper flaring.

"Rhetorical, right?" Agent Tompkins deadpanned.

"Oh, good one, Agent Tompkins," I said, then sat back in my chair, resolved to mind my own business and let the conversation play itself out.

But the Chief noticed the look on my face and leaned forward with his elbows on the desktop.

"What is it?" he said.

"I know someone else who knew where the spare set of keys was kept," I said softly.

"Who?" the Chief said.

"Our former chief of police."

"Jackson? Don't tell me you think he's involved in this?" the Chief said, frowning.

"No, not Jackson," I said. "But don't you think it's a bit of a coincidence it was Jackson's store that got George out of the station."

"Holy crap," the Chief said, his eyes wide. "Wow. I can certainly make that work."

"I'm not following," Agent Tompkins said, glancing back and forth at us.

"Jackson's in the process of selling his store," I said. "To a man who's relocating from Texas."

"Interesting," Agent Tompkins said, sitting back in his chair and mulling it over.

"And given everything going on at the southern border these days, maybe he decided it would be a lot easier and safer to smuggle people in from Canada," I said.

"And probably more lucrative, too," Agent Tompkins said. "A hundred grand a pop is nothing to sneeze at."

"Son of a gun," the Chief said, glancing at me. "How the heck did you do that?"

"It just popped into my head," I said, shrugging it off. "But running a grocery store would be a great cover."

"And he'd certainly be in the loop about all the local gossip," the Chief said. "All the comings and goings."

"Yeah," I whispered.

"You really think Jackson told the guy about the spare keys?" George said.

"You know how Jackson gets when he starts telling stories," the Chief said. "No detail is too small."

"We need to talk to him," Agent Tompkins said.

"Which one?" the Chief said.

"Both of them. But let's start with Jackson."

"We can drive over to the store," the Chief said.

I shook my head but didn't say a word.

"Have you turned shy in your old age?" the Chief said, again noticing my expression.

"I'm just trying to mind my own business," I said. "I made a promise to my mother."

"It's never stopped you before," the Chief said.

"I've never been pregnant before," I said with a shrug.

"Fair point. So, what's on your mind?"

"I'd bring Jackson here without him telling anyone where he was going," I said. "Or better yet, call him and ask him to join you for lunch at C's."

"Good call," Agent Tompkins said. "If the guy buying the store is involved in the smuggling ring, let's not tip him off we might be looking at him."

"Yeah, I like it," the Chief said, nodding as he reached for his phone.

"I need to make a call," Agent Tompkins said. "And if you thought Betty was freaked out by what happened to Roger Smith, just wait until she hears about Walter."

"Should I call Rooster and let him know his cousin is on the loose?" I said.

"It probably can't hurt," Agent Tompkins said, then spoke into the phone. "Hey, Betty. It's me. You're never going to guess what happened."

Chapter 13

I ended my call with Rooster just as Millie returned with our food. She removed three steaming ramekins from a tray and carefully arranged them in front of us. I stared lovingly at my shepherd's pie and nodded my thanks.

"Be careful," Millie said, sliding the serving tray a few feet down the bar. "They just came out from under the broiler."

"It looks like Charlie has outdone himself," Chef Claire said as she spread her napkin across her lap.

"You didn't make it?" I said.

"No, it's my day off," Chef Claire said, swiveling around on her stool to take a look around the half-filled lounge. "Decent crowd for a weekday in November." Then she swung back around and poked several holes in her shepherd's pie with her fork.

"Oh, my word," Josie said, fanning her mouth frantically. Tears formed in her eyes and she gulped down a large drink of water. "Hot."

"What part of just came out from under the broiler didn't you understand?" Chef Claire said, shaking her head. "Are you okay?"

"Yeah, I'm fine," Josie said, wiping her eyes.

"What are you doing?" Chef Claire said, glancing over at me then following my eyes into the dining room.

"Just trying to keep an eye on the conversation Jackson is having with the Chief and Agent Tompkins," I said before focusing on my lunch.

"Do you know what they're talking about?" Chef Claire said as she dipped her fork into the shepherd's pie.

"They're asking him some questions about the guy who's buying the store," I said.

"Because?" Chef Claire said, then took a bite and savored it. "Good stuff. My compliments to the chef."

"It's great," Josie said, nodding.

"I think there's a chance he might be involved in the smuggling ring operating around here," I said.

"I'm going to need a bit more, Suzy," Chef Claire said, frowning as she set her fork down and folded her hands in front of her on the bar.

I glanced around to make sure I wouldn't be overheard then spent the next few minutes reviewing the morning's events. When I finished, I took a bite of shepherd's pie and waited for questions.

"Coke Bottle escaped?" Josie whispered, leaning in close.

"Yeah. Sometime during the night," I said. "And he definitely had help."

"He shot his partner?" Chef Claire said.

"It certainly looks that way," I said. "Freddie said the guy has been dead since yesterday. Coke Bottle probably took him out before he came over to collect the reward money."

"But how is the guy buying Jackson's place involved?" Chef Claire said.

"TBD," I said with a shrug. "If, in fact, he is involved."

"I'm so glad we spend our lives working with dogs," Josie said, taking a break to wipe her mouth. "People can be such a disappointment."

"Yeah," I said, nodding as I snuck another look into the dining room where the conversation was heating up. "I sure wish I could hear what they're talking about."

"Did you forget your microphone?" Josie said.

"Funny," I said. "But that thing works great, huh?"

"It does," she said, resuming her attack on the shepherd's pie.

"Hang on," I said, staring into the dining room. "It looks like Jackson is leaving."

"And he doesn't look very happy," Chef Claire said.

We watched Jackson zip his coat as he headed for the door and departed without a goodbye wave. I wolfed down a couple bites of my lunch then hopped off the stool.

"You're not going to finish that?" Josie said.

"Knock yourself out."

"You can count on it."

"I'll see you guys in a bit," I said, heading straight for the table.

Chief Abrams and Agent Tompkins both looked up when they saw me approach. The Chief pulled a chair back and motioned for me to sit down.

"From the look on his face when he left," I said, settling into the chair. "I'm gonna guess the conversation didn't go well."

"No, Jackson isn't very happy with either of us," the Chief said.

"He's worried his buyer is going to get spooked and walk away from the deal?" I said, reaching for a piece of bread and dredging it in olive oil.

"Among other things," Agent Tompkins said, finishing the last of his shepherd's pie. "Mainly, I think we hurt his feelings."

"By insinuating he's brought a criminal into our midst?" I said, glancing back and forth at them.

"I thought I was being subtle," the Chief said with a frown.

Agent Tompkins laughed.

"Probably not the word I would use," he said. "But don't worry about it, Chief. The question had to be asked."

"Where did you leave it?" I said, then polished off the last of the bread.

"We really didn't get a chance to come up with a game plan," Agent Tompkins said. "Jackson said he needed some time to think about it. We'll circle back with him later. This guy, Joshua, isn't going anywhere at the moment."

"As long as he doesn't get spooked," the Chief said.

"We'll be fine, Chief," Agent Tompkins said.

"So, what's next?" I said.

"Well, I need to huddle with Betty. And I want to take another look at the list of ships who are scheduled to pass through here over the next several days," Agent Tompkins said. "Do you mind giving Rooster an update about his cousin, Chief?"

"Happy to do it."

"He's on his way over," I said. "I talked to him a few minutes ago."

"Did you tell him what happened?" Agent Tompkins said, raising an eyebrow at me.

"No, I just told him you guys had some news for him," I said, then noticed the Chief staring at me. "What is it? Did I spill?"

"No, that's not it," he said. "I just can't believe how well you're behaving. Usually, by now, you'd be up to your neck in this thing."

"Think of me as a consultant," I said, laughing. "Besides, you guys know exactly what you need to do next."

"Enlighten me," the Chief said.

"Find Coke Bottle," I said with a shrug.

"Easier said than done," Chief Abrams said. "I wouldn't have a clue where to start looking. And I'm sure he's gone to ground somewhere we won't find him. He can't be that stupid."

"We are still talking about Walter, right?"

They both laughed then spotted Rooster making his way to our table.

"Hey, Rooster," Chief Abrams said. "Have a seat."

"Hi, folks," he said, settling into his chair. "Suzy said you have something to tell me."

"It's about your cousin," Agent Tompkins said.

"Let me guess. He didn't recover from last night's dust-up, and you need me to identify the body," Rooster said, sounding half-serious.

"He escaped last night," Chief Abrams said softly.

Rooster stared at the Chief then shook his head.

"How hard is it to keep an eye on a guy who took a beating like that?" Rooster said, obviously surprised and annoyed.

"He had help," the Chief said.

"Really, Chief?" Rooster said. "What the hell is wrong with George?"

"He got duped," the Chief said.

"By Walter?" Rooster said, shaking his head again. "Impossible."

"That's where the part about him having help comes in," the Chief said.

"Thanks for clarifying," Rooster said, scowling at the Chief.

126

"It gets worse," Agent Tompkins said. "It looks like Walter killed his partner."

"What?"

"Yeah, the guy got shot in the living room at your house on Willander," the Chief said. "The place is gonna need a good cleaning. Sorry, Rooster."

"Damn," Rooster said, then exhaled loudly.

"And you'll probably need to replace the rug in front of the fireplace," Agent Tompkins said.

"You guys are full of good news today," Rooster said. "When can I get over there to take a look at the damage?"

"You might want to give us a day or two," Agent Tompkins said. "I'll let you know."

Rooster nodded and sat back in his chair. He folded his arms across his chest and repeated his head shake.

"Do you have any idea where your cousin might have gone?" Agent Tompkins said.

"Not off the top of my head. But the two spots where he was hiding were familiar to him," Rooster said. "Walter's pretty predictable. And lazy. My guess would be he's going to end up in another place he knows."

"Like your cabin in the woods where we found him the last two times our paths crossed?" I said.

"I seriously doubt it," Rooster said. "Even Walter can't be that stupid. Let me give it some thought, and I'll let you know what I come up with."

"Thanks, Rooster," Agent Tompkins said.

"What sort of manhunt are you guys putting together?" I said.

"You're pretty much looking at it," Agent Tompkins said.

"What?" I said, frowning.

"The Chief and I talked about it. And we decided to keep things lowkey for the moment," he said, making furtive eye contact with Chief Abrams.

I thought about his comment then grinned at them.

"You don't want anybody to know you screwed up. That's it, isn't it?"

"Maybe that's part of it," the Chief said, chagrined.

"But most of it deals with not blowing the smuggling investigation," Agent Tompkins said, quickly changing the subject. "If we start sending a bunch of cops and FBI agents out on a search mission, people are going to notice."

"People we don't want to spook," the Chief said.

"And we need Walter to keep doing whatever it is he's working on," Agent Tompkins said.

"Even though he's wanted for murder?" I said.

"Yeah," Agent Tompkins said eventually. "Even though he's a murder suspect."

"You're kind of rolling the dice, aren't you, Agent Tompkins?"

"Maybe a little," he said, toying with his knife and fork. "But sometimes you have to do it."

128

"What are you going to do if he kills somebody else?" I said.

"Probably polish up my resume," he said with a shrug. "Or deal with being transferred to North Dakota." He pushed his chair back and got to his feet. "If you'll excuse me, I need to give Betty a call and get an update."

We watched him head for the front door then sat quietly for several moments. Eventually, Rooster broke the silence.

"I'm going to head out to my cabin just to make sure the idiot didn't go there."

"You want some company?" I said.

"Not from you."

"Harsh," I said, laughing.

"You know what I mean," Rooster said. "If Walter did shoot the guy, he's completely freaked out. And there's no telling what he might do if he sees somebody approaching the cabin."

"Okay," I said, nodding.

"And your mother would kill me if she found out I let her pregnant daughter tag along."

"There is that."

"I'll go with you," the Chief said. "I'm the one who let him get away. It's the least I can do."

"I agree," Rooster said, glaring at the Chief. "And bring your idiot deputy along with you. Maybe between the two of you, you'll be able to shake the bumbling small-town cop label."

Then Rooster turned to me and smiled. "For the record, *that's* what harsh looks like."

Chapter 14

I grabbed Sammy's outstretched hand and climbed into the passenger seat of the van. He waited until I got settled in then gently shut the door.

"Are you sure you don't want some help?" he said through the open window.

"No, we'll be fine," I said. "Jackson will give us a hand with the heavy stuff. But thanks for the offer, Sammy."

"Okay, just give me a call if you need me," he said, then waved and headed back inside the Inn.

Josie started the engine then glanced over at me.

"You all set?"

"Lead the way," I said, pointing out the windshield.

"You do know that Jackson would have been more than happy to deliver everything to the restaurant, don't you?"

"I do."

"But you want a chance to talk with this Joshua guy."

"Nothing gets past you."

"Just try to control yourself, okay?" Josie said as she turned left out of the parking lot.

"I'll see what I can do," I said, making a face at her.

We made the short drive to Jackson's store and parked in back near the loading dock. We climbed out and entered through the back door and made a quick right into Jackson's office. Joshua Williams was sitting at the desk and scrolling through a document on his computer screen. He looked up when he heard my soft knock on the open door and smiled.

"Suzy and Josie, right?" he said, getting up to shake hands with both of us.

"Guilty as charged," I said. "Is Jackson around?"

"No, he said he had a headache and was going to take the rest of the day off," Joshua said.

"I'm sure he does," I whispered.

"What?"

"Nothing," I said. "We're here to pick up an order."

"He mentioned you'd be stopping by," Joshua said. "And he said he had it ready out on the loading dock."

He walked past us motioning for us to follow him.

"Are you getting the hang of things?" I said as we made the short walk.

"I'm getting there," he said over his shoulder. "But it's a lot to deal with. This is the first time I've been here by myself. Trial by fire and all that." He came to a stop next to three stacks of boxes and frowned as he looked around the loading dock. "This must be it."

"It is," I said, surveying the boxes.

"Jackson mentioned you guys were big eaters, but I gotta say, this is nuts," he said, laughing. "That's a ton of food."

"It's for the restaurant," I said, laughing along. "These are the stuffing supplies for Thanksgiving dinner."

"Is there a visiting army coming into town I don't know about?"

"I guess time will tell," I said. "No, we serve Thanksgiving dinner for all the local residents who don't have other plans or are alone for the holidays."

"What a nice thing to do," he said, genuinely impressed.

"It's our third year doing it," Josie said. "You should come. It's a lot of fun."

"Geez, I don't know," he said. "I've got a ton of things to take care of on Thursday."

"Is your family coming in for the holidays?" I said.

"No, unfortunately not. They're not going to make it up here until Christmas. Trying to sell the house in Texas and packing. You know the drill."

"I do," I said, nodding as I quickly compared the stacks with the list Chef Claire had given us. "But we're doing three different seatings during the day. You should try to make one of them. The food's great."

"I'll do my best," he said. "Let me help you get this stuff loaded."

The three of us lugged and loaded the boxes into the back of the van. I got off easy and was assigned the task of carrying the bread. When we were done, Joshua closed the van door and wiped his hands on his jeans.

"Okay," he said. "I'm sure the store has an account with your restaurant."

"We do," I said. "Thanks for your help, Joshua. And welcome to Clay Bay. I hope you like it here. It's certainly not Texas."

"No, it's not," he said. "But I sure do love the River."

"As soon as spring gets here, we'll take you fishing," I said. "Unless you'd like to try your hand at ice fishing this winter."

"Standing on the ice waiting to catch a fish?" he said. "I am looking forward to living in a colder climate, but maybe I'll ease my way into that one."

"Good call," Josie said.

"Well, if you'll excuse me, I need to make a phone call before I close for the day."

"We'll let you go," I said, extending my hand. "Thanks again for your help. And try to make it to Thanksgiving dinner if you get a chance."

"I'll do my best," he said, then waved at both of us and headed toward his office.

"He seems nice," Josie said.

"He does. Disarmingly so."

"You mind driving?" Josie said, then tossed me the keys.

I climbed in and started the van then drove toward the back of the parking lot. About a hundred feet away from the store, I came to a stop next to a stretch of pines. I put the van in park and glanced out the windshield.

"This should work," I said, climbing out of the van. I looked around the dim light and nodded to myself. "It's plenty dark enough."

"What are you doing?" Josie said, staring at me.

"Just a little snooping."

"Of course. Dumb question."

I grabbed my duffel bag from the back seat and rummaged through it. Moments later, I climbed back into the van and attached a small device to the driver side mirror.

"Really?" Josie said, staring in disbelief at me.

"He said he needed to make a phone call," I said, turning the device on.

"And you thought you'd just listen in?" Josie said, obviously annoyed.

"Hey, if he is involved in the smuggling ring, wouldn't it be good to know?"

"He's probably calling his wife and kids."

"If he is, then I'll turn it off," I said, handing her an earpiece.

"That looks like a different one from last night," she said, leaning over to take a closer look at the device attached to the mirror.

"It is," I said, nodding. "It's a laser microphone. And it's capable of going through windows. It works off vibrations. I'm not exactly sure how, but it's really cool. The Feds use them all the time."

"Good for the Feds," Josie said.

"Shhh," I said, turning up the volume.

Moments later, I heard Joshua Williams' voice through the earpiece. I glanced over at Josie, and she nodded back at me.

"That thing is good," she said. "It's like he's in the next room."

"Yeah. Shhh."

"This is nuts," Josie said, pulling a bag of bite-sized from her pocket and offering it to me. I waved it off and focused on the man's voice. "I'm sitting in a parking lot at night eavesdropping on a stranger. I so need to find a boyfriend."

"Shhh."

"Did you have any problems getting the idiot out of jail?" Joshua Williams said. "Good. Where is he?"

"I wish we could hear the other side of the conversation," I said, glancing over.

"Shhh," Josie said, now listening closely.

"He's probably laying low," Joshua continued. "I'm sure he'll turn up. Has Roger checked in today? What? He got shot? No wonder the idiot is staying out of sight...Oh, I see. Roger's dead. Well, I guess that solves one problem and creates another, huh? Yeah, I'm sure we'll figure it out. Just as long as Thursday goes smooth, we'll be fine." Then he laughed. "We'll have all winter to figure it out. Talk to you later."

Josie and I removed our earpieces, and I released the microphone from the outside mirror. I tossed the items back into

136

the duffel bag and zipped it shut. Then I glanced over at Josie and did my best not to look smug.

"Okay, you were right," Josie said. "He's involved."

"Yeah, I had a hunch," I said. "Interesting he hadn't heard Roger Smith was dead."

"Well, he did say he'd been working at the store all day," Josie said, unwrapping a bite-sized. "What did he mean by his comment about having all winter to figure it out?"

"My guess is he was referring to finding a replacement for Roger," I said, deep in thought. "He was the guy who handled the paperwork."

"What?"

"The new identities. You know, passports, driver's licenses, stuff like that."

"Got it," Josie said. "This has to be the last run of the year before winter gets here."

"It certainly sounds that way," I said. "Okay, let's get this stuff delivered."

"And we might as well have dinner there," Josie said, sliding the bag of bite-sized into her pocket. "What's Chef Claire making as the special tonight?"

"I forgot to ask. Does it matter?"

"It never has before."

I was about to close my window when I caught a glimpse of someone standing outside the driver side door. Then I got a close look at the pistol inches away from my face.

"Good evening, ladies."

I flinched and held both hands up then gently rested them on the steering wheel.

"Hey, Walter," I finally managed to get out. "Long time, no see."

"Yeah, I've missed you too," he said.

"What on earth happened to your face?" I said.

"I slipped in the shower," he said, glancing around the immediate area. "What are you doing here?"

"We had to pick up some stuff for Thanksgiving dinner," I said, glancing over at Josie.

"Must be my lucky day," he said, waving the pistol. "Get out of the van."

We both complied and slowly climbed out. We stood next to each other and waited for further instructions. And waited some more. Coke Bottle stood a few feet away pointing the gun at us, deep in thought.

"Problem?" Josie deadpanned.

"Quiet. I'm trying to think."

"About what?" I said.

"Whether I should shoot you here, or take you with me as hostages," he said as a simple statement of fact.

"Do we get a vote?" Josie said.

"Shut up," he said, waving the pistol at her.

"Isn't killing one person enough for the day?" I said. "I mean, you don't want to overdo it, right?"

Coke Bottle squinted at me and pressed his glasses tight against the bridge of his nose.

"What are you talking about?"

"Roger. Roger Smith," I said.

"What about him?" Coke Bottle said.

"You shot him," I said, frowning. "You did shoot him, didn't you, Walter?"

"I didn't shoot nobody."

"Anyone," Josie said.

"Don't start."

"Yeah, probably good advice," she said, keeping a close eye on the gun.

"Roger got shot?" Coke Bottle said, apparently having difficulty processing the information.

"That's the rumor," I said.

"Why would anybody want to shoot him?" he said.

"I was hoping you might be able to tell us," I said. "You really didn't do it?"

"Like I just told you, I didn't shoot nobody."

Josie let his poor grammar pass without comment and glanced at me.

"You know what this means, right?"

"I do," I said, nodding.

"What are you talking about?" Coke Bottle said, glancing back and forth at us.

"Just thinking out loud," Josie said.

139

"Well, keep it to yourself," he said. "Where did he get shot?"

"Just to clarify, are you talking about body parts or geographic location?" I said.

"What?" he said, squinting hard in my direction.

"Never mind," I said. "They found his body in the living room at Rooster's place on Willander. One in the chest, one in the head."

"He got shot today? At Rooster's place?"

"The cops think it was sometime last night," I said, studying his face. "That's gotta hurt, right?"

"Yeah, it looks nasty," Josie said, nodding.

"Just shut up and let me think," Coke Bottle said.

"Let us help you with that, Walter," I said.

"What?" he said, giving me a puzzled look.

"If you didn't shoot him, and judging by the look on your face, I think I believe you, then there's only one logical explanation for what's going on."

"Absolutely," Josie said, nodding.

Coke Bottle frowned then motioned with the pistol for us to continue.

"You're being set up for murder, Walter," I said softly.

"I am?"

"It certainly looks that way," I said, then glanced at Josie. "Wouldn't you agree?"

"You took the words right out of my mouth," she said, flashing a coy smile at him. "Now who would want to do that to you, Walter?"

"If you'd asked me that question a few minutes ago," he said. "I would have said Roger."

"Ironic," Josie whispered.

"What?"

"Nothing," she said. "This isn't good, Walter. Somebody is obviously out to get you."

Coke Bottle's blank stare never left his face as he continued to ponder the possibilities. Then he nodded vigorously.

"It's Rooster," he said.

"Rooster?" I said, surprised.

"Interesting choice," Josie said.

"Yeah, he's always hated my guts."

"Actually, I think he just hates some of the choices you've made, Walter," I said.

"It don't matter," he said. "Yeah, this situation has got Rooster's name all over it. It's exactly the sort of crap he'd try to pull."

"Not to be difficult, Walter," Josie said, gently bouncing on her toes. "But what's next? I'm freezing my butt off."

"Hold your horses," he said, then had a thought. "I guess it's your lucky day, too."

"How's that?" I said.

"I'm not going to shoot you."

"Good call, Walter," Josie said.

"At least not right now," he said. "You two are tight with Rooster, aren't you?"

"We are," I said.

"That means he wouldn't want to see anything bad happen to you."

"No, he wouldn't," I said.

"And I bet he'd be willing to make a trade," Coke Bottle said.

"What sort of trade are we talking about, Walter?" I said.

"A trade of freedom," he said, breaking into a smile. "My freedom for yours."

"I can live with that," Josie said, glancing over at me.

"It's a start," I said with a shrug. "Okay, Walter. What do you need from us?"

"We're going to take a little boat ride."

"Tonight?" Josie said.

"Can you think of a better time?" Coke Bottle said, glaring at her.

"June?"

"You're pretty funny for somebody with a gun pointed at her. I need to search you." He glanced back and forth at us then waved the gun in my direction. "Let's start with whatever you've got stuck under your coat."

"What?" I said, confused.

"The lump under your coat. What is it?"

"That's my daughter Maxine," I said, scowling at him. "And I'd prefer it if you didn't refer to her as a lump."

"You keep your kid under your coat?" he said, bewildered.

Josie was unable to stifle her snort.

"I'm pregnant," I said, shaking my head.

"Oh," he said. "Congratulations. Give me your phones." He slid them into his pocket then focused on me. "Put your hands over your head."

I did and he patted me down before focusing on Josie.

"Your turn," he said. "Put 'em up."

Josie raised her arms and Coke Bottle began his search.

"Hey, watch the hands," she snapped. "Do you really think I'd hide a gun there?"

"Sorry," he said, then took a step back. "Okay, get in the van."

We both nodded and climbed in. Coke Bottle opened the side door and sat in the backseat. He slid the door shut and leaned forward.

"Just don't do anything stupid and you'll be fine," he said.

"Got it," I said. "Where to?"

"The dock at Island Wonderland," he said.

"The resort?"

"Yeah, it's shut tight for the winter, but they haven't got all their boats out of the water yet."

"Okay," I said, starting the engine and exiting the parking lot. "Where are we going?"

143

"You'll see," he said, finally noticing what we had in the back of the van. "Geez, that's a lot of bread."

"We're feeding a lot of people on Thanksgiving," I said, looking at him through the rearview mirror. "You should come."

"I'm busy Thursday," he said. "But remind me to grab a couple loaves before we get on the boat. I doubt if there's anything to eat where we're going."

"Perfect," Josie said, shaking her head.

I continued to drive slowly until we hit the highway. I cleared my throat to get Josie's attention. When it failed, I repeated it and added a cough. Finally, she glanced over at me. I snuck a peek in the mirror then pointed the little finger of my right hand at the glove compartment. She gave me a small smile and unzipped her coat.

"So, what brings you back to town, Walter?" I said, making eye contact with him in the mirror.

"Nothin'."

"Sure, sure."

I kept one eye on Josie as she slowly removed a small plastic container from the glove compartment and slid it inside her coat. She zipped it up then settled back into her seat.

"Can I ask you a question, Walter?" Josie said.

"If you must."

"How bad is your eyesight?"

"It's bad," he grunted. "But as long as I wear my glasses, I can get by. It's 20/100."

"20/100, corrected?" Josie said, turning around to look at him.

"Yeah," Coke Bottle said. "Without my glasses, I'm pretty much screwed."

"It must be tough," Josie said.

"I get by," he said, then leaned forward and pointed. "Take a right onto that dirt road."

I did as commanded and we made our way down the service-road entrance to the resort. I parked near the dock and turned the van off.

"Okay, nice and easy," Coke Bottle said, climbing out. He watched us closely as we got out then pointed at the boathouse. "Lead the way."

We made the short walk, and Coke Bottle flipped the light switch. I spotted three boats gently rocking in their slips.

"Let's take the big wooden one," he said.

"Nice boat," I said, grunting as I tried to reach down to untie the bowline.

"Let me get that," Josie said.

"Thanks," I said, then looked at Coke Bottle. "You want to drive?"

"Me? At night? Not my favorite," he said. "You drive."

"Okay," I said, slowly working my way onto the boat.

"The key is under the seat cushion," he said.

"You must have been a Boy Scout, Walter," I said, locating the key.

"What?"

"You know, always be prepared and all that crap," I said, firing up the engine. It came to life with a throaty roar.

"No, I couldn't cut it with the Boy Scouts," he said, stepping down into the boat. "I got kicked out for stealing merit badges."

"Why doesn't that surprise me?" Josie whispered, sliding into the seat next to me.

"Where are we going, Walter?"

"Do you know Fortune Island?"

"I do," I said, putting the boat in gear and slowly heading out of the boathouse. "It's a beautiful island. Do you know the owners?"

"A bit," he said, relaxing when we hit open water. "I used to be the caretaker. But that only lasted one summer."

"Why's that?" I said, glancing over my shoulder.

"You sure do ask a lot of questions."

"Just making chitchat, Walter," I said with a shrug.

"Let's say I found something more fruitless and leave it at that."

"Full," Josie said, glancing over her shoulder.

"What?"

"Fruitful. You found something more fruitful."

"Really?" I said, glancing over at her.

"How's he gonna learn?" she whispered. Then she shivered when a blast of frigid air hit us. "Geez, it's brutal out here."

146

"It is," I said. "And I need to pee."

"Me too. Full speed ahead, Captain."

Chapter 15

Fortune Island started out as a multi-acre patch of granite and pine trees but had been transformed into a summer playground by a wealthy family from somewhere in the Midwest. I'd never met them, but their taste in homes and landscaping was indisputable. Josie and I led the way up the winding path to the main house perched on the apex of the island but came to a stop when Coke Bottle, holding the pistol in one hand and a flashlight in the other, stopped us in our tracks.

"Make a right," he commanded.

We did and followed a branch in the path to a smaller structure a couple of hundred feet away. Coming to a stop directly in front of the door, we glanced at each other as we waited for further instructions.

"Guest cottage?" Josie said.

"That would be my guess," I said, following the beam of the flashlight.

Coke Bottle rummaged through a collection of flower pots scattered on the porch and finally found what he was looking for. He held the key up as he headed for the door.

"How many hiding places do you have around here, Walter?" I said, genuinely interested in the answer.

"Enough," he said with a grunt as he opened the door and waved us in. He closed the door behind us then shined the flashlight on a large couch. "Have a seat and make yourself comfortable. We're gonna be here awhile."

We sat down and watched Coke Bottle light three kerosene lamps. The room slowly came into view, and we got our first good look at our surroundings. The cottage was small but well-appointed. We both nodded our approval.

"I love the color scheme," I said.

"Me too," Josie said. "What color is that?"

"I think it's teal."

"It works well with the white trim," she said. "And this couch is comfy."

"Shut up," Coke Bottle snapped as he rubbed his forehead. "Just be quiet and let me think." He paced back and forth then came to a stop. "Do either one of you know how to build a fire?"

"Yeah. Good call, Walter," Josie said, getting to her feet. "I'll take care of it."

"Nice and slow," he said, finally sitting down across from us.

"I need to pee, Walter," I said.

"Me too," Josie said over her shoulder as she built a pile of kindling.

"Get the fire going and then we'll see," Coke Bottle said.

"I'm not joking, Walter," I said. "I'd hate to ruin this beautiful couch."

"Don't worry. They can afford a new one."

I heard the crackle of the fire and soon felt the heat it was throwing off. Josie waited until she was sure the fire would hold, then added a log and sat back down.

"You did good," Coke Bottle said to Josie.

"Girl Scouts," she said with a shrug. "Got my campfire merit badge the first year."

"I stole mine," he said. "I think I've still got it around somewhere."

"I'd love to sit here and listen to you two reminisce about your scouting days, but I'm busting here, Walter."

"All right," he said, getting to his feet. "There's a half-bath off the kitchen with no windows. Use that one."

"Right about now I'm willing to use the kitchen sink," I said, holding my knees together as I made the short walk.

Josie followed me, trailed closely by Coke Bottle who was carrying one of the lamps. He set it down on the kitchen table and watched me closely as I made my way toward the bathroom.

"Don't take too long," Josie said, pressing her knees together.

A few minutes later, I emerged from the bathroom feeling much better. Josie made a beeline for the door. When she came out, she gave me a small nod, and we headed back to the couch. The fire was now roaring, and we removed our coats. Coke Bottle sat down deep in thought.

"Penny for your thoughts," I said.

"Huh? What?"

"You seem to have a lot on your mind, Walter," I said.

"I'm thinking."

"Yes, I can see that. You want some help?"

"I'm trying to figure out a way to get Rooster over here without him tipping off the cops," he said, scratching the stubble on his chin with the tip of the pistol.

"That's a tough one," I said, nodding.

"Well, you know what I always say," Josie said, removing a bag of bite-sized from her pocket. "It's hard to think on an empty stomach."

"What have you got there?" he said, staring at the bag in her hand.

"Bite-sized Snickers," she said, gently shaking it.

"I like those," he said, nodding.

"Then here you go," she said as she tossed one to him. Then she offered the bag to me. "You want some?"

"Maybe just one," I said, reaching into the bag.

"Slacker," she said, popping one into her mouth and devouring it.

"Ugh," Coke Bottle said, making a face as he swallowed. "I think I got a bad one."

"What's the matter?" Josie said.

"Bitter," he said. "Must have gotten a bad nut."

"Yeah, I hate when that happens," she said. "Here, try another one."

Coke Bottle caught it, then quickly unwrapped it and tossed it back. He chewed and nodded.

"Much better," he said. "Toss me another one."

"Just take the bag," she said, tossing it to him. Then she leaned in close and whispered. "My work is done."

"How much did you use?" I whispered back.

"All of it."

"Really?"

"Yeah."

"Won't that kill him?"

"Nah," she said, shaking her head. "He'll just take a nice long nap."

I glanced over at Coke Bottle who was rapidly working his way through the bag of bite-sized. Josie frowned but said nothing.

"Would you like us to call Rooster?" I said eventually.

"I'm still thinking it through," he said, stifling a yawn.

"Okay," I said, studying him closely. "Take all the time you need."

"Thanks for giving me your permission," he said, then popped the final chocolate morsel and crumpled up the empty bag. "I'm still hungry. Damn. We forgot to bring the bread."

"It's always something, right?" I said.

We settled back on the couch and waited for the acepromazine to start working. Ten minutes later, Coke Bottle's eyes were half-closed and his head bobbed. The movement woke him up and he yawned.

"Man, I'm beat," he said. "Tell you what. Let's give Rooster a call and then I'm going to tie you two up so I can catch a little shuteye before he gets here."

"There's no need to tie us up, Walter," I said. "We're stuck on an island. Where are we gonna go?"

"I can't trust you," he said slowly.

Then he nodded off, and his gun fell to the floor. Josie hopped off the couch and grabbed it. She glanced around the room and frowned.

"Okay, he's definitely out," she said, taking another look around.

"What are you looking for?"

"Something to tie him up with," she said, then headed for the kitchen and began rummaging through the drawers. She returned moments later, grinning as she held up a large roll of duct tape. "This oughta do the trick."

She handed me the gun, and I watched as she wrapped duct tape around Coke Bottle's hands and feet. She took a step back to admire her work then continued. She pulled him upright in the chair then wound the tape around him and the chair until he resembled a duct-taped mummy. I laughed at the sight then stood up.

"Good job," I said, taking another look at Coke Bottle. "Okay, now what?"

"Well, I guess we either stay and wait for the cops or get the heck out of here," Josie said.

"I vote for the latter," I said, pulling on my coat.

"Good call," she said. "He's not going anywhere. Grab the keys to the boat," she said, nodding at the coffee table. "Race you to the dock."

"Funny," I said, heading for the door.

"Hang on," she said, approaching the sleeping moron. She removed his glasses and set them on an end table near the door.

"You're bad," I said, laughing.

"I'm not done," she said, grabbing the flashlight then blowing out all three lamps. "Sweet dreams, Coke Bottle."

"He's gonna freak out when he comes to," I said, stepping outside and getting a blast of frigid air.

"We can only hope," Josie said, leading the way to the dock.

We climbed into the boat, and I fired up the engine while Josie untied the lines. She sat down next to me and made herself as small as possible as the cold enveloped us when I accelerated away from the dock.

"I hate running like this at night," I said above the roar of the engine.

"Then slow down," she said, visibly shivering. "I'd rather freeze than go for a swim."

"Yeah, you're right," I said, pulling the throttle back. "There's no hurry."

"We'll pick up the van, make our delivery then sit in front of the fireplace and have some dinner," Josie said.

"Good plan," I said, keeping a close eye on the water in front of us. "We need to call the Chief."

"Yeah, he'll be able to get a jump on things," she said, patting her pocket. "Damn."

"What's the matter?"

"Our phones," she said, shaking her head. "Coke Bottle still has them."

"Crap," I said. "You want to go back and get them?"

"Not really," she said. "Let's just get to the restaurant. The Chief's probably there."

"Yeah, I think he said he was having dinner with Agent Tompkins," I said, then laughed. "That guy is like a lovesick puppy around her."

"He is," Josie said, laughing along. "Chef Claire likes the guy."

"I know. But she hates the idea of long-distance relationships."

"Can't blame her for that," Josie said.

I nodded then shivered as another blast of frigid air pounded us.

"I need you to do something," I said, hunkered down behind the windshield.

"What's that?"

"Remind me to take the boat out of the water on Friday. This is ridiculous."

Chapter 16

We entered through the kitchen door and found Chef Claire in front of a broiler keeping a close eye on a couple of steaks. She glanced over when she heard us come in and frowned.

"What did you do? Decide to bake your own bread?"

"Sorry," I said. "We had a bit of…an adventure."

"An adventure?" she said, removing the steaks from the broiler and placing them on plates. "Hey, Charlie. Can you finish prepping these two New Yorks?"

"Sure, Chef Claire," Charlie said. "Hi, guys. How's it going?"

"Better now that we're inside," Josie said, still shivering from the boat ride.

"What happened?" Chef Claire said, folding her arms as she leaned against one of the counters.

We gave her the short version, and she listened closely with a frown plastered on her face.

"He kidnapped you?"

"Yeah, I guess you could say that," Josie said. "But we're fine."

"And mum's the word to you know who," I said, maintaining eye contact to emphasize my point.

"Got it," she said, nodding. "Will I get a chance to use my bat on him?"

"Probably not," I said. "But we appreciate the thought. Is the Chief here?"

"Yeah, he and Agent Tompkins are having their dessert in the lounge. I take it you haven't eaten."

"No, and I'm starving," Josie said. "I'm going to start with some soup."

"Definitely," I said, nodding.

"I made a batch of hot and sour today," Chef Claire said. "People seem to be enjoying it."

"What a shock," Josie said. "Two bowls, please." Then she glanced at me. "What are you going to have?"

"Funny," I said, gently shoving her toward the door. "We'll see you in a bit. The fire is calling my name."

We entered the lounge and headed for the bar where Millie was chatting with Sammy and Jill. All three greeted us and gave us the once-over.

"Did you guys change your hair?" Sammy said.

"Yeah, it's called windblown-chic," Josie said, making a face at him.

"What can I get you guys?" Millie said.

"Coffee, please," I said. "No, make that a hot chocolate."

"Perfect," Josie said. "Me too."

"We ordered soup," I said. "We'll be eating in front of the fire. Thanks, Millie."

We sat down on a couch across from the Chief and Agent Tompkins who were both working their way through huge pieces of chocolate cake.

"We were wondering where you were," Chief Abrams said, then noticed the look Josie was giving his dessert. "You want a bite?"

"No, thanks," she said. "I'll wait. That fire feels great."

"It certainly does," I said, removing my coat.

"Are you okay?" the Chief said, studying me closely.

"It's been a day," I said, then started to tell them the story of our evening.

"Hang on. Walter kidnapped you from the parking lot at Jackson's store?" the Chief said.

"Yeah," I said.

"What the heck was he doing at the store?" Agent Tompkins said. "Pretty risky move on his part."

"I imagine he was looking for some help from this guy Joshua Williams."

"Interesting," the FBI agent said.

"Hang on," the Chief said. "What were you doing hanging around Jackson's parking lot?"

"We were picking up supplies for the stuffing," I said.

Josie snorted.

"Shut it," I said, but couldn't miss the looks the Chief and the FBI agent were giving me. "And we were doing a little snooping."

"From the parking lot," the Chief said.

"Yeah," I said, nodding. "Okay, while we were at the store, Joshua said he had to make a phone call. We decided to listen in."

"Excuse me?" Josie said. "We?"

"Okay, it was my idea," I said with a shrug. "But she was listening too."

"You were hiding inside the store?" the Chief said.

"No, we were in the van," I said, glancing up when a server arrived with our soup. "Thanks, Bobbie."

"Enjoy," he said, then departed.

I ate a spoonful, nodded my approval, then had another. Josie was making quite a racket as she made short work of her bowl.

"If you can keep it down a bit, I'll continue with the story," I said, staring at her.

"Talk louder," she said, not even glancing up.

"So anyway, we were in the van listening in on his phone call," I said.

"How is that possible?" Agent Tompkins said.

"You were using that new laser microphone," the Chief said. "Weren't you?"

"Yeah," I said, beaming at him. "It works great." Then I had a thought. "Hey, where's Betty? It's not like her to miss dinner."

"She got a call this afternoon," Agent Tompkins said. "Somebody broke into her house last night. She drove up to check out the place and talk to the cops. She'll be back in the morning."

"Geez, that sucks," Josie said, placing her empty soup bowl on the coffee table. "Did the cops say what they took?"

"I don't think they went over it on the phone," Agent Tompkins said, then focused on me. "Let's get back to you eavesdropping on Joshua Williams."

"Sure," I said, then slid a spoonful of soup into my mouth and savored it.

"Please don't take this the wrong way, Suzy," Agent Tompkins said. "But if you manage to screw up this investigation, we're going to have a serious problem."

"Really?" I said, eyeing the FBI agent. "No offense, Agent Tompkins, but if my math is correct, I'd say, without my help, you'd be a lot worse off."

"I see," he said, spreading his arms as he returned my stare. "Then, by all means, enlighten me."

"I'll be happy to do that, Agent Tompkins," I said, my voice turning guttural.

"Easy," Josie said, placing a hand on my arm.

"I'm fine," I said. "Whose idea was it to use the offer of a reward to smoke Walter out in the first place?"

"Yours," Agent Tompkins whispered.

"And do you think you would have caught him without my help?"

"No, not at that moment," the FBI agent said. "But I'm sure we would have."

"Probably," I said, nodding as I conceded the point. "But then Walter escaped. Whose *screw up* was that?"

"His," Agent Tompkins said, nodding at the Chief.

"How's the view from under the bus, Chief?" Josie said.

"I'll let you know in a minute," the Chief said, glaring at the FBI agent.

"Sorry, Chief," Agent Tompkins said. "That was our screw up."

"There you go," I said. "I figured out a way to catch him. You let him get away. Suzy, one. Cops, zero."

"Knock it off," Josie said firmly.

"I'm fine," I said, glancing over at her. "You know, Agent Tompkins, it's not so much what you say, it's the smug, snotty way you do it that ticks me off. You should take a page from Betty's book about how to talk to people."

"Well, if there's anyone who would recognize smug and snotty it would be you," he said, glaring at me.

"You son of a-"

"Whoa," the Chief snapped. "That's enough. Both of you need to chill. We're on the same team here."

Agent Tompkins and I maintained our death stares then we both relaxed. I nodded at him and forced a small smile.

"I'm sorry."

"Yeah, me too," he said. "It's just that we've got a lot riding on this investigation."

"Well, we have good news for you," I said.

"How's that?" the Chief said.

"We managed to catch Walter," I said, then couldn't resist taking another jab. "Again."

"What? Where is he?" Agent Tompkins said, leaning forward.

"He's duct-taped to a chair on Fortune Island," Josie said. "And sleeping like a baby."

The Chief and Agent Tompkins stared at each other.

"You just left him there?" the FBI agent said.

"He's not going anywhere," I said. "We were freezing."

"And very hungry," Josie said.

"And there was no way we were going to try to carry Coke Bottle to the boat," I said.

"Let's back up a bit," the Chief said. "What happened after you ran into him at the store?"

Josie and I recounted our adventure. Before we could finish, Agent Tompkins held up a hand to stop us.

"He knew where the key was?"

"He did," I said. "Coke Bottle said he used to be the caretaker, but my guess is he's been back there recently. Since it's the third different place he's used as a hideout, he obviously has a bunch of spots ready to go."

163

"Yeah," the Chief said, then frowned. "Hang on a sec. Walter's a big guy. How the heck did you manage to get away?"

"With a bite-sized Snickers," I said.

The two men stared at each other again. The Chief focused on us and motioned with his hand for us to continue.

"We're probably going to need a little more."

"Josie worked her magic," I said, beaming at her. "It was beautiful."

"Aren't you sweet."

"Now that's how you talk to somebody, Agent Tompkins," I said, flashing a smile at him.

He flinched but said nothing.

"After Coke Bottle checked us for weapons in the parking lot, Josie managed to grab the first aid kit we keep in the glove compartment."

"Yeah," Josie said. "Since we never know what we might run into when we're picking up strays or rescues, I like to keep a supply of acepromazine in the kit."

"The sedative?" the Chief said.

"That's the one," Josie said.

"And that's why he's currently sleeping like a baby," I said.

"How did you manage to inject him?" Agent Tompkins said.

"We didn't," I said. "That's where the bite-sized comes in."

"Again," the Chief said, thoroughly confused. "I'm definitely going to need a bit more."

164

"I went to the bathroom and emptied a syringe of acepromazine into one of the bite-sized," Josie said.

"Through the wrapper," I said, grinning.

"And Walter ate it?" Agent Tompkins said. "Just like that?"

"Hey, who can say no to a bite-sized?" Josie deadpanned.

The Chief and I laughed.

"How long will he be out?" Agent Tompkins said.

"Probably hours," Josie said. "But don't worry. He's not going anywhere. He's wrapped tighter than an Egyptian mummy."

"She used the whole roll of duct tape."

"Do you know where Fortune Island is?" Agent Tompkins said to the Chief.

"I do," he said, nodding. "At this time of night, it'll take us about half an hour to get there."

"Bundle up," Josie said.

"Definitely," I said, nodding in agreement.

"Okay," Agent Tompkins said, slapping his thighs as he got to his feet. "Let's do this, Chief."

"Aren't you forgetting something?" I said, glancing back and forth at them.

"Oh, that's right," the Chief said, reaching for his wallet. "The check. Let me get this one, Agent Tompkins."

"Not the check," I said, frowning at the Chief. I glanced at Josie. "Unbelievable."

"Yeah, I gotta agree with you on that one," she said, laughing.

"What did we miss?" Agent Tompkins said.

"Don't you want to know what Williams said on his phone call?"

"Oh, the phone call," Agent Tompkins said. "I completely forgot."

"You were able to hear him?" the Chief said.

"Like I said, the laser mic works great," I said.

"Well...?" Agent Tompkins said, staring down at me.

"He's definitely involved," I said, then looked at Josie who nodded in agreement. "And it's happening on Thursday."

"On Thanksgiving Day," Agent Tompkins said. "That's smart. The day when everybody is sitting around the house eating and drinking."

"And trying not to pay attention to what's going on in the outside world," I said.

"Okay," Agent Tompkins said, nodding. "Good stuff. Well done, ladies. Top notch work. Really, top notch."

"You're welcome," I deadpanned. "And you have my word I'll do my best not to *screw up* your investigation."

"Knock...it...off," Josie whispered.

"I'll let you know how it goes," the Chief said, pulling on his coat.

"Do us a favor," I said. "We left our phones over there."

"Okay, we'll grab them," he said.

166

"Good luck," I said.

We watched them head out then perused the menu.

"I thought they'd never leave," Josie said as she scanned the menu. "I'm starving. What are you going to have?"

"Those New Yorks looked pretty good," I said, sliding the menu away.

"Good call," she said. "For sides, I'm going with the scalloped potatoes and succotash."

"Oooh, I'm in," I said, glancing around to catch the eye of our server. Then I stared off into the distance as my neurons flared.

"What is it?" Josie said. "You've got that look."

"I was just wondering if Coke Bottle's hiding places aren't as random as they might appear."

"That's what you're thinking?"

"At the moment, yeah."

"I'm so glad I don't have your brain," she said, shaking her head.

"Yeah, you probably should be thankful."

"Remind me to mention it on Thursday."

Chapter 17

The next morning, I was in my office with a map of the Thousand Islands spread across my desk. Chloe, my Aussie Shepherd, made several attempts to get comfortable in my lap but my ever-expanding belly made it difficult. Eventually, she gave up and sprawled out on the couch and was soon sound asleep. I stood and placed my hands on the desk as I leaned forward to study the map. I grabbed a pen and drew circles around the town of Rockport on the Canadian side, then circled the three spots Rooster's cousin had used as hiding places.

I glanced up when Josie, dressed in her scrubs, entered and headed for the couch. She gently lifted Chloe's head and slid underneath her.

"Slow day," Josie said. "I thought I'd come here and bug you for a while. What are you doing?"

"Mapping out Coke Bottle's hiding spots to see if there's a pattern."

"Any luck?"

"Not yet," I said, studying the map. "I just got started." I glanced up when I heard the knock. "Come on in."

Rooster entered and waved to both of us. Chloe woke up and thumped her tail on the couch. Rooster spent a few minutes petting her then sat down in a chair on the other side of the desk.

"What a good girl," he said, looking at Chloe who was already resuming her morning nap.

"Thanks for stopping by," I said, sitting down.

"No problem," he said. "It gave me something to do other than watch cable news."

"That stuff will rot your brain, Rooster," Josie said.

"Yeah, I'm on overload from ten different versions of the same story," he said. "What's up?"

"We had a little run-in with your cousin last night," I said.

"A run-in? Where?"

He listened closely as Josie and I told him the story. When we finished, he nodded and sat back in his chair.

"Well done. Where is he now?"

"I'm sure he's back in jail and getting hit with a whole bunch of questions," I said.

"He's lucky that's all he's getting hit with," Rooster said. "Did you get him to confess to the murder?"

"No," I said, shaking my head. "In fact, he seemed genuinely surprised by the news. He didn't kill the guy."

"Probably only because he didn't get the chance," Rooster said. "What's the deal with the map?"

"I'm trying to see if there's some sort of pattern to Walter's hiding places," I said, getting to my feet.

Rooster got up from his chair and walked around to my side of the desk. He studied the four circles I'd made then scratched the stubble on his chin.

"I'm not picking anything up," he said.

"Me neither," I said. "But there must be a pattern here somewhere."

"Why are you so insistent?" Josie said. "We're talking about Coke Bottle here."

"I know," I said. "And he's certainly not the brains behind whatever this thing is. My guess is the ringleader told him to find hiding places that met their needs."

"Well, if there's one thing Walter knows, it's the River," Rooster said. "He's a River Rat through and through."

"I know," I said, nodding. "And that's why I'm sure the spots he picked out weren't random. But what the heck is it?"

"How long has this smuggling ring been operating?" he said.

"The Chief says it's probably been working the area since last spring," I said. "At a minimum."

"It would be easy to pull off something like this in the summer," Rooster said. "With the number of tourists and boats out on the River, you could pretty much run the length of the River without anybody paying much attention. As long as you didn't do anything stupid to attract the attention of the cops or Coast Guard."

"Especially if you've been given new identities," Josie said.

"Yeah. And if you were smart enough to only smuggle in small groups at the same time," Rooster said.

"Now, that's interesting," I said, deep in thought. "Betty said the FBI is sure this is going to be the final run before winter. A big run."

"They better hurry," Rooster said. "It's snowing at the moment."

"Wonderful," Josie said, shaking her head. "We haven't even hit Thanksgiving."

"But if they've been doing small runs up to this point, and using a bunch of different boats and entry points, this last run might mean they had to change their usual strategy," I said.

"And that's why they needed someone with Coke Bottle's expertise?" Josie said.

"Yeah, I can make that work," I said.

"Me too," Rooster said, studying the map. "Rockport makes sense as the drop-off spot on the Canadian side."

"That's what I thought at first," I said, pointing at one of the circles. "But Jackson's camp isn't very close."

"Maybe Coke Bottle couldn't come up with a better option," Josie said.

"No, there are tons of places," Rooster said.

"Well, he definitely picked spots he's familiar with," I said. "Jackson's place, yours, and Fortune Island where he used to work."

"But those three are all off the table now," Rooster said. "They wouldn't use any of them now."

"No, I'm sure they won't," I said, frowning. "So, there must be at least one more." Then my neurons flared. "Hang on. Let's go back to what you said about only smuggling in small groups."

"What about it?" Rooster said.

"I think they're going to have to do one big pickup in one location now that the other three spots can't be used," I said. "But I think the original plan was to do several small pickups along the way."

"I'm confused," Josie said.

"If they're bringing in small groups at a time, maybe they planned on stashing each group at a different location. You know, half a dozen or so at a time."

"And then they would use one boat to collect all of them and head for the drop-off spot on the mainland?" Rooster said.

"It sounds weird," I said, frowning. "But when you think about it, it's pretty clever. If one of the locations was discovered, you might still be able to slip away with the ones who weren't caught."

"Or the logistics of dealing with six at a time is more manageable," Rooster said.

"That makes even more sense," I said, then flinched.

"Don't do that," Josie said, startled.

"Sorry."

"What is it?" Rooster said.

"They're not using Rockport for the drop-off," I said, pointing at the map. "That's the spot, right there."

"I know that area," Rooster said. "It's some sort of nature preserve. Or at least that's what the Canadian government is thinking about doing with it."

"Yeah, thick woods, several marshy inlets, and a decent access road," I said. "And Walter would be familiar with it, right?"

"I'm sure he is," Rooster said. "He used to trap when he was a kid. And that's a perfect spot for muskrat."

I grabbed my pen and circled the spot then drew straight lines from the three hiding places Coke Bottle had used.

"Look at that," Rooster said. "I bet it's almost the same distance from all three."

"It sure looks like it," Josie said, looking over my shoulder. "But you said they need a fourth location."

"Yeah," I said, focused on the map. Then my mouth dropped open. "Wow."

"What?" he said.

I drew a circle around an island thereby completing the pattern.

"Holy crap. I don't believe it," I said.

"That's your mom's place," Rooster said. "Serenity Island."

"That's the one," I said, then chuckled and shook my head. "She renamed it after I hit my teenage years. She finally decided it was the only place she could get some peace and quiet."

"I remember," Rooster said with a grin. "We've had some great parties over there."

"Yeah," I said, nodding. "And the house is certainly big enough to hold a couple dozen people."

"Easily," he said. "And there's a deep-water dock on the channel side if they need it."

"You'd need a pretty big boat to transport two dozen people," I said.

"You thinking some sort of yacht?" Josie said.

"No," I said, shaking my head. "A yacht would stick out too much. But a nice cabin cruiser would do the trick. And it wouldn't attract too much attention. There's always some folks wanting to sneak in one last trip before winter."

"And a cruiser could be docked in hundreds of spots up and down the River," Rooster said.

"We need to swing by the station and talk to the Chief," I said.

"Maybe I'll get a chance to have a little chat with my cousin," Rooster said.

"It's good to have dreams," Josie said.

Chapter 18

We found Chief Abrams and Agent Tompkins sitting across from each other at the desk. Whatever heated conversation they were having stopped as soon as they saw us. Agent Tompkins' expression remained dark as he nodded at us and the Chief could only summon a quick greeting.

"Have we come at a bad time?" I said, glancing back and forth at them.

"Yeah," the Chief said. "It's not a good morning."

"What's the matter?" Rooster said, sliding into a chair.

"Your cousin," the Chief said.

"What did he do now?" Rooster said, unconsciously clenching his fists.

"He escaped," the Chief whispered.

"What?" I said.

"Impossible," Josie said. "When we left, he was mummified."

"Yeah, we saw the remains of the duct tape," the Chief said. "You used enough to stop a train."

"Somebody cut him loose?" I said.

"It certainly looks that way," the Chief said. "A pair of garden shears were on the floor near the fireplace."

"But how the heck did anybody know he was there?" Josie said with a scowl.

"We've been wondering the same thing," Agent Tompkins said, finally cooling down enough to join the conversation. "Did he make a phone call while you were in the van or on the boat last night?"

I looked at Josie and we both shook our heads.

"If he did, I didn't notice," Josie said.

"I don't think he did," I said.

"He probably sent a text," the Chief said.

"What about his phone records?" I said, focusing on Agent Tompkins. "That should be easy enough to check. You know, since you guys can read my license plate from outer space."

"That's the NSA and CIA," Agent Tompkins said, not taking the bait. "And we already checked after the incident with the dog. Walter doesn't have a cellphone."

"They must all be using burners," I said. "So, Coke Bottle managed to send a text to someone telling them he was heading to Fortune Island."

"With us in tow," Josie said, glancing over at me.

"There's a cheery thought," I said. "I guess we're lucky we aren't at the bottom of the River." I looked back and forth at the Chief and FBI agent. "Joshua Williams?"

"That's our best guess at the moment," Agent Tompkins said. "But we don't want to confront him yet."

"Because you don't want to spook him?" I said.

"Not until we absolutely have to," Agent Tompkins said. "But it may come to that at some point."

"We don't have a lot of time," the Chief said. "Thursday is right around the corner."

"I know that, Chief," Agent Tompkins said, his temper flaring.

"Relax," the Chief said, waving the agent's anger away. "We'll figure something out."

"I think we can help you with that," I said, then heard the FBI agent exhale loudly. "Problem, Agent Tompkins?"

"You two should have stayed there and waited for us."

"And do what?" I snapped. "Get shot by whoever showed up to cut him loose?"

"Easy guys," Chief Abrams said, reaching into his desk drawer. "Well, there is one thing working in our favor. Walter's going to have a tough time making the run on Thursday without these." He tossed Coke Bottle's glasses on the desk. "I've never seen anything like them."

I stared at the thick lenses that dwarfed the wire frame.

"They forgot to take his glasses."

"Nothing gets past you."

"Shut it," I said, gently punching Josie on the shoulder.

Josie grinned at me then leaned forward and slid the glasses on. Her head appeared to be on a swivel as she glanced around the room briefly then removed the eyeglasses and handed them back to the Chief.

"Geez, I'm dizzy," she said, rubbing her eyes.

"Do you think he's got a spare set, Rooster?" the Chief said.

"Knowing Walter, I doubt it. He told me one time how expensive his glasses were. And I'm sure he prefers to spend his money on more important things."

"Like beer and Slim Jims?" Josie said.

"Exactly," Rooster said, grinning at her.

"We have to figure out a way to get them back to him," I said.

"We?" Agent Tompkins said, giving me a dead-eyed stare.

"It's a figure of speech, Agent Tompkins," I said without looking at him.

"Why don't I believe you?"

"Will you two knock it off?" the Chief said, his voice rising. Then he frowned. "I probably should have asked earlier, but why are you here?"

"I came along hoping I could have a quick word with my cousin," Rooster said with a shrug.

"And I thought you'd have doughnuts," Josie said.

"Sorry to disappoint you," the Chief said.

"It's okay, Chief," Josie said. "I'm trying to cut back."

The Chief laughed then focused on me.

"I came by to share something with you," I said, holding up the cardboard tube the map was in.

We all looked up when the door opened, and Betty Smithsonian entered looking frazzled.

"Sorry it took me so long to get here," she said, removing her coat. "It's snowing in Ottawa, and the roads are a mess."

"Is it heading this way?" Josie said.

"Sad to say, it looks like it," Betty said.

"Lovely," Josie said, shaking her head.

"Is everything okay at your house?" I said.

"Yeah, it'll be fine," Betty said. "The cops think it was a gang that's been operating in the city for a while. They got my stereo and TV and some jewelry. Most of it's covered by insurance, but it's a major pain in the neck to deal with."

"Yeah, I'm sure it is," I said, nodding sympathetically. "Sorry, Betty. That's the last thing you need to be dealing with at the moment."

"Stuff happens," she said with a shrug as she sat down. "So, what's going on?"

"We were just lamenting the disappearance of Walter," the Chief said.

"Still? That was a couple of days ago, guys," Betty said, laughing. "Time to move on, wouldn't you say?"

The Chief and Agent Tompkins looked at each other then the Chief gestured for the FBI agent to bring her up to speed. Agent Tompkins spent the next few minutes hitting the high points of yesterday's events then fell silent.

"You captured him again, but he got away?" Betty said.

"Suzy and Josie, two. Cops zip," I whispered.

"Don't start," Josie whispered back.

"Okay. Like I said, stuff happens," Betty said. "So, we're back to where we were when I left yesterday. But we've confirmed this guy Joshua is involved. That's gotta help, right?"

"We need to play that card carefully," Agent Tompkins said.

"Sure," Betty said, nodding. "We don't want to spook him." She focused on Agent Tompkins. "You want me to swing by the grocery store and see if I can kick up some dust bunnies?"

"It might be worth a shot," Agent Tompkins said. "But make sure he thinks you're only there to shop."

"Do I look like an idiot?" Betty said, now cranky.

"Sorry," he said. "I'm running on no sleep."

"Don't worry about it," Betty said.

"The glasses," I said.

"What about them?" the Chief said.

"This is the chance to return them to Walter," I said. "If Betty can figure out a way to drop them off somewhere in Williams' office, he'll make sure Coke Bottle gets them."

"He'll need them to make the run on Thursday," Betty said. "Good call. Yeah, I can do that."

"Glasses or not, it won't matter if we can't figure out *where* the run is going to take place," Agent Tompkins said.

"That is the problem," Betty said, nodding.

Josie looked at me and slowly swept an arm toward the cops.

"You're on," she said.

"What?" I said, coming back to the moment.

"That's your cue to talk," she said.

"Oh, right," I said. I removed the map from the tube and unfolded it on the desk. It started to roll itself back up, and the Chief placed coffee mugs on each corner to hold it in place.

"What the heck is this?" Agent Tompkins said, studying the map.

"It's the location of where the drop-off is going to happen," I said.

"And you know this how?" he said.

"Horrible syntax, Agent Tompkins," I said.

"You really know how to make friends, don't you?" he said, looking up from the map to scowl at me.

"Usually," I said. "But it looks like I might need to make an exception for you."

"Suzy, please stop," the Chief snapped, then nodded at the map. "Just take us through it."

I did.

When I finished, I sat down and waited for questions. Agent Tompkins went first.

"That's your mother's place?"

"It's one of them," I said. "What do you think?"

"I think it's brilliant," Betty said. "And you're sure Walter knows his way around that area?"

"I am," Rooster said. "Despite his shortcomings, and there are many, Walter was the perfect choice for the job."

181

"I suppose he was," Betty said, nodding. "Do you think that's where he went after he escaped last night?"

"I'd bet a paycheck on it," the Chief said, then focused on the FBI agents. "You think we should take a little trip over to Serenity Island?"

I sat quietly with a deep frown on my face. Eventually, the Chief noticed and glanced over.

"What is it?"

"If it were me, I'd just leave him alone," I said. "Let him relax for a couple of days. Let him think he's outwitted the cops."

Agent Tompkins looked at Betty then the Chief.

"Yeah, I like it," he said, finally managing to smile at me. "Well done, Suzy."

"I had help."

"Still," Betty said. "It's a nice piece of work putting that together. There's just one thing. Why four different locations?"

"Probably for insurance," Agent Tompkins said. "If they have been running small groups at a time, it makes sense to use multiple locations."

"But with the other three locations blown, her mom's place is the only option they've got left," Betty said.

"Unless they have more," Agent Tompkins said.

"No, that's where it's going to happen," Rooster said.

"Why do you say that?" Agent Tompkins said.

"Because Walter has been to Serenity Island, and he knows how comfortable it is. Once he gets his butt settled down over there, he won't move until it's time to do the run," Rooster said.

"He's been there before?" the Chief said.

"Yeah, I brought him along to a party one time," Rooster said. "Probably not the smartest thing I've ever done."

"I don't know, Rooster," the Chief said. "It might turn out to have been a brilliant move." He looked at me. "How do you want to handle your mom?"

"With kid gloves," I said, laughing.

"You want some help with the conversation?" the Chief said.

"No, we'll be fine, Chief."

"We?" Josie said, frowning. "Uh, I think I'll pass."

"I wasn't talking about you," I said, grinning at Rooster. "I was talking about him."

"Me?"

"He's your cousin."

"Don't remind me."

Chapter 19

My mother paused, mid-bite. She wiped her mouth then sipped wine and sat back in her chair.

"It's odd you mention Serenity, darling."

"Why's that, Mom?"

"Because I just included it this morning in the trust fund I'm setting up for my granddaughter."

"Trust fund?" I said, genuinely surprised. "You're setting up a trust for her?"

"Of course," she said, grabbing her fork. "Aren't you?"

"I thought I might wait until I actually had her, Mom," I said, taking a bite of my cheeseburger. "Please tell me you didn't get her a pony."

"Don't be silly, darling," my mother said, giving me a coy smile. "Not until she's eight. Maybe ten."

"You got a college picked out?"

"I'm thinking Ivy League," she said, shrugging. "But we have some time to decide."

"Unbelievable."

Rooster laughed as he went back to work on his beef stew.

"Why do you want to talk about Serenity?" my mother said.

I put my burger down and launched into the story. My mother listened closely, occasionally nodding, often frowning.

But she didn't interrupt and continued working her way through her spinach salad as I talked. When I finished, I nibbled on a pickle as I waited for the inevitable questions.

"I need to ask you something," she said eventually.

"Sure, sure."

"Not you, darling," she said, fixing a hard stare on Rooster. "Has my daughter once again defied my order to keep her nose out of things that are none of her business? And if she has, Rooster, have you willingly gone along with it?"

"No, Maxine," Rooster said, shaking his head. "This one just sort fell into her lap. She didn't go looking for it."

"But now she's in it up to her neck, right?"

"Well, maybe not her neck," Rooster said, going for funny without success.

"I see," my mother said.

"But there's nothing to worry about," Rooster said. "She's not going to get anywhere near Serenity when this thing goes down."

"I suppose it's a start," my mother said, then focused on me. "You figured it all out?"

"I had help," I said, shrugging. "But it's pretty clear what's going to happen on Thursday."

"Smuggling people," she said, shaking her head. "What next?"

"They're smuggling people with money."

"And that makes a difference?"

"To them, probably," I said.

"I was referring to the disgusting practice of human trafficking."

"I know what you were talking about, Mom," I said. "I just wanted you to know your island was involved."

"I see," she said, taking another sip of wine. "Thank you, darling."

"You're thanking me?" I said with a frown then glanced at Rooster who also seemed taken aback by her response.

"Of course," she said. "I appreciate you letting me know."

"Has the doctor changed your meds?"

"Funny, darling."

"I can't believe how calm you are," I said. "I thought you'd go ballistic."

"As long as you didn't go looking for trouble and promise to stay out of the way, I don't have a problem with this one. Apart from the fact that despicable creature is probably stretched out on my new couch eating Cheetos as we speak. No offense, Rooster."

"None taken," Rooster said.

"How many people will be inside my house?"

"A couple dozen," I said. "But not for long. And I'm sure the cops will need to go through the place when it's over."

"Wonderful," she said with a frown. "Where will the cops be?"

"They'll probably drop some off onshore, and the rest will be in boats near the island," Rooster said. "At least, that's how I'd handle it."

"Yeah, that makes sense," I said, nodding.

"Okay," my mother said, tossing back the last of her wine. "Just one more thing, Rooster."

"What's that?"

"You're going to replace everything your idiot cousin breaks or steals, right?"

"Absolutely," he said.

"Okay," she said, getting up. "Now, if you'll excuse me, I need to run to a meeting. Thank you for lunch, darling. Tell Chef Claire the salad was perfect."

She leaned down to give me a hug and a kiss then left with a wave.

"What the hell was that?" I said.

"She's mellowing with age," Rooster said with a shrug.

"I'm gonna stick with the meds theory."

"Your little girl is going to have a very special life."

"Yeah, I know," I said. "Let's just hope she doesn't find out how special it is until she's old enough to handle it."

"That's the approach your mom used with you," Rooster said.

"She did. Thinking back, she did a great job with that."

"She did a great job, period. And the proof is sitting right across from me."

"Aren't you sweet."

"I have my moments," he said, reaching out to gently squeeze my hand. "And speaking of sweet, let's have some dessert."

Chapter 20

I entered the back door of the Inn and began my normal routine of saying hello to all the dogs. The number of permanent residents had recently dropped to around fifty due to a successful adoption event we had staged in October. But several people had boarded their dogs while they were traveling over Thanksgiving. I opened the door to Tiny's condo, and the enormous Great Dane slowly made his way to all fours and approached. I hugged him and gently probed his hips, a problem area for him the past few months.

"I think the anti-inflammatories Josie prescribed are helping."

I looked around and spotted Sammy standing at the door.

"Good morning," I said, still probing Tiny's hips with my fingers. "He does seem a bit better."

"I'm worried how he's going to handle the cold this winter," Sammy said as he approached and rubbed the dog's head.

"Yeah, me too," I said. "Do what you can to minimize his outside time. I know he loves playing in the snow, but we don't want him overdoing it. Do we, Tiny?"

The Great Dane wagged his tail vigorously as we left the condo and closed the door behind us.

"How's the Tibetan doing?" I said, coming to a stop in front of the next condo.

"He's better," Sammy said. "But the poor guy is still on edge."

"He's been traumatized," I said, kneeling down to greet the cocker spaniel who was standing on his back legs and wagging his tail. He licked my hand when I reached inside the condo to scratch his ears. "One day he's living a pampered life roaming around several acres, then the next he gets tossed into a van and forced to spend all his time with Coke Bottle."

"Yeah, I'd be cranky, too."

"Then he finds himself on an island and ends up here surrounded by sixty other dogs," I said. "He's completely disoriented."

"He'll be fine once his owner gets here," Sammy said.

"Yeah, I'm sure he will." I glanced down the line of condos until I saw the Tibetan. He had spotted me and was giving me an intense stare. "If looks could kill."

"It must be weird for you," Sammy said. "You know, a dog that doesn't like you."

"I made him look bad the other day," I said, shaking my head at the memory. "And Wilbur is too smart to forget it."

"But the good news is that he and Chloe have bonded," Sammy said.

"Is he still searching the perimeter of the play area for an escape route?"

"Every time he goes out to pee," Sammy said. "He's tenacious. But Chloe keeps herding him away from the fence when he starts digging."

"Let him dig. The only thing he's going to hit is concrete. He's not going anywhere."

"I'm surprised he hasn't tried to jump the fence."

"Seven feet?" I said, giving the idea some thought. "If he can manage that, I suppose he's entitled to get away. Is he doing better with the other dogs?"

"I try to minimize the number of dogs he's outside with. A lot of them are pretty twitchy when he's around."

"Good job, Sammy. Is Josie around?"

"She's finishing up an annual exam at the moment. And I think that's all she has scheduled today."

"We've hit the winter doldrums."

"Jill and I were talking last night," Sammy said. "And we think we're going to take you up on the offer to stay at your place on Grand Cayman."

"Knock yourself out," I said. "And feel free to take some friends along. There's plenty of room."

"Thanks, Suzy. We appreciate it. Okay, I need to get back to work."

I spent the next hour saying hello to the rest of the dogs and thought about doing the same with the Tibetan. But he emitted a guttural growl when I approached. I held up my hands in mock surrender and headed for my office. Chloe hopped off the couch when I entered and greeted me with kisses and a tail wagging in double-time.

"That's how it's done, Wilbur," I said as I rubbed her ears.

I sat down and removed a stack of bills and receipts from a drawer and began writing checks. A half-hour later, Josie entered and stretched out on the couch. Chloe took advantage and draped herself across her lap.

"Where's Captain?" I said, happy for the interruption to the dreaded paperwork.

"Up at the house. He's a little punky today," Josie said. "I caught him chewing on a dead fish yesterday. I don't think it agreed with him. And as soon as he feels better, I need to give him a bath. He stinks."

"Are you done for the day?"

"Yeah. And I doubt if we're going to see much activity over the holiday," she said, getting up to pour herself a cup of coffee. "You want one?"

"No, I've had my limit," I said, closing the checkbook and putting it away. "Should we cook tonight, or do you want to go to the restaurant?"

"Oh, let's go to the restaurant," she said, gently stroking Chloe's back. "Chef Claire's on a hot streak at the moment."

"Good call," I said. "I think I'll invite the Three Amigos."

"Because you just have to know the latest about the investigation?"

"I'm dying to hear their game plan for Thursday."

"Just try not to send Agent Tompkins into orbit," Josie said, sitting up. She laughed as Chloe grumbled about having to move and waited until she got resettled. "Excuse me, your majesty."

"Demanding little minx, aren't you?"

Chloe glanced up at me with her head cocked then stretched out again with her head in Josie's lap.

"What is it with you two?" Josie said.

"I don't know," I said, frowning. "I think it's the superior attitude he gives off at times. One minute, he's sweet as can be, the next he comes across as a total jerk."

"He's just territorial about his work," she said with a shrug. "I imagine it's the way they're trained to be."

"Betty's not like that at all."

"She's younger than Agent Tompkins. Maybe the Bureau is starting to recruit a new breed of agents," Josie said. "You know, a kinder, gentler FBI."

"Something like, hold still, this is going to hurt me a lot worse than it is you?" I said with a grin.

"There you go," she said. "Just try not to make him mad, okay?"

"I'll do my best."

We spent the rest of the day futzing around the Inn. When we ran out of things to do, we headed to the registration area and played Scrabble with Sammy and Jill until closing time. Josie and I walked up to the house to take care of the dogs then showered and dressed for dinner.

We entered C's through the kitchen and spotted Chef Claire sitting at the chef's table with Charlie, her sous chef, and two servers. They were playing cards and glanced up when they heard us come in.

"Busy night, huh?" I said.

"Deader than roadkill," Charlie said, playing a card.

"Is the Chief here yet?" I said.

"Haven't seen him," one of the servers said, glancing up at us. "How are you guys doing?"

"Great, Bobbie," I said, then turned to Josie. "You want to wait for them in the lounge?"

"Lead the way," she said.

We sat at the bar chatting with Millie. I glanced around the empty lounge then took a sip of my club soda. I gently rubbed my stomach and sighed.

"What's the matter?" Josie said.

"Oh, it's nothing. I always get a little melancholy this time of year. Especially when I see an empty room like this."

"Don't go there," Josie whispered.

"Yeah, you're right," I said, blinking back the tears. "Sorry."

"Don't apologize," she said, patting my hand.

"This is where I would usually have a glass of wine," I said, dabbing at my eyes with a tissue.

"Yeah, I know," she said. "How about a bite-sized?"

I laughed and shook my head.

"No, thanks. Maybe after dinner. There they are."

The three cops entered through the front door and removed their coats. Josie and I got off our stools and met them halfway.

"I take it we're not going to have a problem getting a table," Chief Abrams said, taking in the empty restaurant.

"No, we pretty much have our pick, Chief," I said, giving him a hug. "Hi, Betty. Agent Tompkins."

"How are you guys doing?" Agent Tompkins said.

"Just peachy," Josie said, motioning for everyone to follow her into the dining room. "How about a table near the fire?"

"Works for me," the Chief said. "It's cold tonight. I can't imagine how brutal it's going to be out there on the River on Thursday. They're still predicting snow and a lot of wind."

We settled into our chairs and Bobbie and Chef Claire emerged from the kitchen. Bobbie passed out menus then took our drink orders and headed off.

"Hi, Chef Claire," Betty said. "What's good tonight?"

"Really, Betty?" Josie said, not even bothering to open her menu.

"Yeah, dumb question," Betty said, then laughed. "What's the soup?"

"I made a seafood chowder I think you'll like," Chef Claire said. "And we also have Minestrone."

"What's the special?" Chief Abrams said.

"I went comfort food tonight. We've got two lasagnas," she said. "A sausage and meatball, and a vegetarian with mushrooms and spinach."

"Can I do a half and half?" Josie said.

"I think I can make that work," Chef Claire said.

"Great idea," Betty said. "Make that two."

"You want to join us?" I said to Chef Claire.

"Maybe for coffee and dessert. We already ate."

We finished ordering and Chef Claire headed back to the kitchen as Bobbie returned with our drinks. After he departed, we sat quietly sipping and basking in the warmth of the roaring fire. Eventually, I couldn't resist any longer and got the ball rolling.

"So, how was your day?" I said, going for casual.

The Chief laughed and glanced back and forth at the FBI agents.

"I told you."

"She is predictable," Agent Tompkins said, shaking his head. "Well, if you must know."

"And she does," Josie said over the top of her wine glass.

"Shut it," I said, then leaned forward and focused on Agent Tompkins.

"You were right," he said softly.

"About him buying a boat?" I said, surprised.

"Yeah, Williams bought himself a forty-five-foot cabin cruiser," Agent Tompkins said.

"I still can't believe we didn't think of that," Betty said.

"Don't remind me," Agent Tompkins said.

"When did he buy it?" I said.

"About six months ago," he said. "From a marina on the Canadian side."

"But he hasn't been driving it, has he?" I said.

"No, it's been sitting at the marina since he bought it," Agent Tompkins said. "But a couple of weeks ago, someone stopped by to take delivery."

"Let me guess," I said. "A big guy with really thick glasses."

"That's the one," Betty said.

"Any sign of the boat?"

"Nope," Agent Tompkins said.

"Did you manage to get Coke Bottle's glasses back to him?" I said.

"I did," Betty said. "Or at least as close as I could. I slipped them into Williams' coat while he was in the store chatting with the current owner. Jackson, right?"

"Yeah," the Chief said.

"Hang on," Josie said. "Isn't he going to wonder how the glasses ended up in his coat?"

"I imagine he will," Betty said. "But if he's the guy who rescued Walter from the island, and we're almost positive he was, he might not give it a lot of thought."

"Maybe he'll think Walter somehow managed to put them there when he was being rescued," the Chief said.

"Coke Bottle should have been out of it," Josie said. "I gave him a major dose."

"Maybe he has a big tolerance," Agent Tompkins said.

"I don't know," Josie said with a frown. "If I were this guy Williams, I'd be suspicious about how the glasses got there."

"Me too," Betty said. "But it was the best we could come up with on short notice."

"Even if he's suspicious, I doubt it will be enough for him to cancel his plans," I said.

"That's what we're counting on," Agent Tompkins said, then focused on Betty. "Oh, I forgot to mention something. I organized a briefing tomorrow afternoon with the state police and Coast Guard folks who'll be helping us out."

"Tomorrow afternoon?" Betty said, frowning.

"Yeah. Is that a problem?" Agent Tompkins said.

"It is," she said. "Do you mind handling the briefing by yourself?"

"Why?"

"I got a call from the Ottawa cops this afternoon," Betty said. "They grabbed a guy trying to unload a bunch of jewelry at a pawn shop. They said it matches the description of the stuff that got stolen from my place. They're holding him until I can get up there and identify it. If it matches, they know they've got the right guy."

"When will you be back?" Agent Tompkins said.

"Late tomorrow night," Betty said. "But I'll be ready to go first thing Thursday morning."

Agent Tompkins thought about it then nodded.

"Sure. Not a problem. I'll handle the briefing. I hope you get your stuff back."

"Me too," Betty said. "There are a couple of pieces that have been in my family for generations."

"How are you going to handle Thursday?" I said.

Agent Tompkins took a few deep breaths then nodded at the Chief.

"We're pretty sure they're going to make the run at night. But just to be sure, we'll have boats in the area during the day."

"People fishing, right?" I said.

"Yeah," the Chief said. "When it starts to get dark, we'll move some other boats in and anchor offshore from your mom's place. If it's snowing like they predict, between the storm and the new moon, there's no way we'll be spotted."

"We'll also drop some folks off on the back side of the island," Betty said. "And as soon as Walter shows up with his guests, we'll swoop in."

"It should work fine," Agent Tompkins said. "I'm sure they'll be lots of cash on hand. And as soon as we match the people being smuggled in with the photos on the counterfeit docs, we'll be able to button this one up in a hurry." Then he had a thought and glanced at Betty. "You still have them in a safe place, right?"

"What?" Betty said, confused.

"The documents we found the day Roger Smith was killed," Agent Tompkins said.

"You said you were going to take them with you," Betty said.

"I did?"

"Yes, you did," Betty snapped. "I asked what you wanted to do with them, and you said you'd take care of them."

"I don't remember," he said with a deep frown. "But there was a lot going on. I probably wasn't paying close enough attention." Agent Tompkins looked at the Chief. "I suppose it's too much to hope you grabbed them."

"No, I didn't touch them," Chief Abrams said firmly. "You both made it perfectly clear they were FBI property."

"Yeah," Agent Tompkins said. "That sounds like something we'd say."

"That means they're still in the bedroom where I found them," Betty said.

"Damn," Agent Tompkins said. "Well, I guess I'll have to head over there in the morning. You mind giving me a ride, Chief?"

"No problem," the Chief said. "I'm just glad you remembered them tonight."

"Me too," Agent Tompkins said, his face flushed with either anger or embarrassment. He caught my eye and maintained solid eye contact. "You got something to say?"

"Dress warm," I deadpanned. "It's going to be cold out there."

He flinched and took a deep breath, his anger now unmistakable. I glanced at Josie who was giving me a big smile.

"Remarkable restraint," she whispered.

"Thanks. I told you I could play nice."

Chapter 21

After dessert and coffee, Agent Tompkins and Betty left the restaurant, their moods only slightly improved after a great dinner. Josie and the Chief followed me to the lounge, and they both ordered an after-dinner drink. I stuck with club soda.

"That was pretty sloppy on their part," I said, then tossed a log on the fire.

"Leaving the ID's behind?" Chief Abram said. "Yeah, he can't catch a break. But stuff like that happens. Especially when you're dealing with dead bodies."

"Do you think the documents are still there?" Josie said.

"They're either still there, or Walter went back to Rooster's place to grab them," the Chief said with a shrug. "Either way, it shouldn't matter. Catching them in the act with the people they're smuggling across the border is what counts."

"Makes sense," Josie said, then glanced at the front door. "Hey. Look who's here."

Jackson and Joshua Williams were in the foyer removing their coats. Jackson spotted us and waved and both men headed straight for us.

"Good evening, folks," Jackson said, his good mood apparent.

"How are you, Jackson?" I said, smiling up at him. "Hi, Mr. Williams."

"Oh, please, call me Joshua," he said. "Hi, Chief."

"How are you doing?" the Chief said, returning the handshake.

"Things are good," Joshua said, then turned to Jackson. "I'll be right back. I need to wash my hands. Those boxes of lettuce were filthy."

He headed off and Jackson watched him go with a huge smile.

"He's going to buy the place," he said. "We're here to celebrate. What's good tonight?"

"The lasagna," we said in unison.

He noticed the frown on my face.

"What's the matter with you?" Jackson said.

"You want to tell him, or should I?" I said to the Chief.

"Go ahead," the Chief said, patting his chest. "I'm still digesting."

"It looks like Joshua is definitely involved in the smuggling ring," I said.

"Don't tell me that," he said, scowling. "This is the first time I've been in a good mood all month. Are you sure?"

"Let's say we'd be shocked if he wasn't," I said.

Jackson looked at the Chief who nodded his agreement.

"Damn," Jackson said. "I finally find a buyer for the store, and he turns out to be a criminal?"

"It's probably better you find out now," I said.

"Why's that?" Jackson said.

"You might end up dealing with the FBI. I'm sure you've heard the term *asset forfeiture*," the Chief said.

"They could seize the store?" Jackson said, his eyes wide.

"And the money he used to pay for it," the Chief said. "But only if you've actually sold it to him."

"That's not fair," Jackson said.

"You'd probably get it back at some point," the Chief said. "But do you really want to deal with something like that?"

"All I want, Chief, is to get out from under the thing and spend my days taking people fishing."

"Find another buyer," Josie said.

"Gee, now why didn't I think of that?" Jackson said. "In case you haven't noticed, potential buyers aren't exactly falling out of trees."

"Don't bark at me," Josie said. "I was only making a suggestion."

"You're absolutely positive?" he said, glancing around. When we didn't respond, he grimaced and shook his head. "What should I do? We're supposed to sign the docs on Friday."

"Just stick with your plan," the Chief said.

"A minute ago, you said don't do the deal, now you're telling me to go ahead? Make up your mind, Chief."

"What I'm saying is stick with the plan," the Chief said. "The situation will sort itself out by Friday."

"And I'm supposed to play dumb and pretend nothing is going on?" Jackson said.

"I'd certainly appreciate it if you would," the Chief said.

"Damn," Jackson said. "I can't believe it." He turned to me. "Do you want to buy a grocery store?"

"Not a chance," I said. "I've seen what all those hours have done to you."

"You think your mom might be interested?"

"Jackson, my mother is a lot of things. But grocery store owner isn't one of them."

"Yeah," he said with a sad shake of his head. "Dumb question."

Joshua Williams returned and focused on Jackson.

"Are you okay?" he said.

"Yeah, I'm fine," Jackson said. "I just got bad news about somebody's plans falling apart."

"That's too bad," Joshua said.

"I'm sure he'll be fine," I said. "Things will sort themselves out soon enough. Do you think you're going to be able to make it to Thanksgiving dinner?"

"You know," Joshua said. "I think I will. I was able to free up some time on Thursday."

"Great," I said, smiling at him. "We'll add you to the list. Which session would you like?"

"What are my options?"

"Eleven, two, or five," I said.

"I'll take the eleven o'clock," Joshua said. "I like to eat early on Thanksgiving. And I have something to take care of later in the day."

"Perfect," I said.

"You ready to eat?"

"Yeah," Jackson said. "I sure hope my appetite returns."

They headed for the dining room. When they were out of earshot, Chief Abrams spoke first.

"I kinda feel bad for the guy."

"Jackson or Williams?" I said, frowning.

"Both of them, I guess," the Chief said. "But Jackson can always find another buyer."

"While Williams is going away for a long time?" Josie said.

"Yeah," the Chief said. "What a tangled web we weave and all that."

"I don't feel sorry for him," Josie said firmly. "He made his own choices."

"Maybe bad isn't the right word," the Chief said, then shook his head. "Sympathetic is probably better."

"You getting soft in your old age, Chief?" I said, grinning at him.

"I don't know. I'm used to watching bad behavior play itself out, but I've never really enjoyed it. You know, dealing with people who choose to do harm to others."

"People choosing to hurt animals is what makes my blood boil," I said.

"You don't say," the Chief said. "I never would have known."

Chapter 22

We said goodbye to the Chief and headed for the kitchen where the staff, despite the empty dining room, were hard at work. Chef Claire looked up from the list she was reviewing when she heard us come in.

"Right on time," she said, checking her list again. "Since you guys did such a great job last year, I've got you on stuffing prep again if that's okay with you."

"Works for me," Josie said. "Tell me again why we're doing this on Tuesday."

"I've been looking for ways to take some of the stress out of Thanksgiving," she said, pointing at a workstation near the walk-in cooler. "We're making as many things in advance as possible."

"Makes sense," I said, then sniffed the air. "I smell gravy."

"We're working on the gravy, stuffing, cranberries, and a couple of casseroles."

"Geez, Chef Claire," Josie said. "You're only cooking for three hundred, what's the rush?"

"Funny," Chef Claire said. "Your onions and celery await."

"Slave driver," Josie said, motioning for me to follow her. "Who's turn is it to chop onions?"

"Yours," I said, pulling an apron on. "I did it last year. My eyes didn't recover until Christmas."

Josie glanced at several boxes stacked next to the workstation.

"That's a lot of onions," she said.

"You have no idea," I said as I rolled up my sleeves and pulled on a pair of plastic gloves. "Okay, time to tear some bread."

I was halfway through the first tray of stale bread and up to my elbows when my phone rang.

"Dang it," I said, removing my gloves and tossing them aside. I answered on the third ring. "This is Suzy."

"Hi, Suzy. It's Bill Franklin."

"Detective Franklin from Ottawa?"

"That's the one. How are you doing?"

"I'm almost back to normal. Thanks for asking," I said, choking back my emotions. "How's Shirley?"

We'd met the detectives when we were in Ottawa and had helped them out on a couple of murder investigations. We'd also watched their relationship develop during that time, and they were now married.

"She's great," he said. "But we're no longer working together. The higher-ups didn't think it was a good idea to have a married couple working as partners."

"I guess that makes sense," I said. "And it gives you a chance to ask the question."

"What question?"

"How was your day?" I said, then laughed.

"Good one," he said. "It's nice to see you've got your sense of humor back."

"So, what is she working on?"

"They've got her heading up a special task force dealing with a gang of thieves operating in the city."

"I heard you're dealing with a burglary ring," I said.

"You've been following the Ottawa news?" he said. "You need a hobby."

"No, someone who's visiting had her house broken into the other day," I said.

"That's too bad," the detective said. "Those guys get around. Shirley's hoping they're able to get a handle on it before the snow arrives. Nobody wants to be chasing them around in the middle of February."

"I think you might have caught a break," I said. "She's heading back up there tomorrow to identify some jewelry the cops think might be hers. They caught a guy trying to pawn it."

"Really? Shirley didn't mention it."

"I think it just happened this afternoon," I said as I watched Josie expertly work her way through one onion after another. "I know you didn't call to talk shop. What's up?"

"I was wondering if you guys are doing Thanksgiving dinner at the restaurant again this year," he said.

"We are. Third year. Why do you ask?"

"Well, we got a couple days off and, if it's okay, we'd like to come."

"Absolutely," I said. "That's right, Canadian Thanksgiving was last month."

"It was," he said. "It was great. We had a bunch of family over. It looks like we've got a nice tradition developing. And Shirley and I were talking about ways to improve the meal next year when we remembered what you guys did down there. And it's a chance to eat Chef Claire's food, right?"

"It is indeed. We'd love it if you guys could join us."

"Are you sure? I know you do it primarily for the local folks. We don't want to impose. And if it's not okay, just so say. You won't hurt our feelings at all."

"Relax, Bill," I said. "We do it for our friends. And you and Shirley are always welcome."

"Thanks, Suzy," he said. "What time are you serving?"

"Eleven, two, and five," I said. "Take your pick."

"Let me check with Shirley when she gets home, and I'll give you a call," he said.

"No problem," I said. "Just let me know as soon as you can. We're trying to finalize the numbers tomorrow."

"Will do. Thanks. Looking forward to seeing you guys."

"Me too," I said. "Talk to you soon."

I set my phone down and grabbed a fresh pair of gloves.

"Detective Franklin, I presume?" Josie said, not glancing up.

"Yeah. He and Shirley are driving down on Thursday."

"Nice," she said. "It'll be good to see them."

"It will," I said, grinning at her. "But it's nothing to cry about."

"Funny," she said, sliding a pile of chopped onions into a large bowl.

I went back to work and five minutes later both our phones chirped in tandem. We looked at each other and frowned, then picked up our phones.

"That's the signal we get when the security system at the Inn is turned off."

"Call Sammy and see if he or Jill stopped by to do something," Josie said, her concern obvious.

I did and he answered immediately.

"Hi, Sammy," I said. "Are you at the Inn?"

"No," he said. "My phone just beeped. I was about to call you. Are you at the house?"

"No, we're at the restaurant," I said, pulling off my gloves.

"I'll meet you at the Inn," Sammy said, then ended the call.

"Let's go," I said, grabbing my coat and keys.

"Right behind you," Josie said.

"What's up?" Chef Claire said.

"The security system at the Inn is off," I said, heading for the door. "We'll give you a call as soon as we know anything."

"Okay, but be careful," Chef Claire said. "You want me to call the Chief?"

212

"No, not yet," I said, exiting through the back door. "It probably just malfunctioned."

"For the amount of money we paid for that system?" Josie said, zipping up her coat as she walked. "Not likely."

We made the short drive and found Jill already inside with all the lights on. Moments later, a shaken Sammy entered from the condo area.

"Wilbur's gone," he said.

"What?" Josie said.

"Unbelievable," I said, doing my best to stay calm. "Are any other dogs missing?"

"It doesn't look like it," Sammy said.

"The house dogs," Josie said, heading for the back door. "I'm going to check on them."

"Okay," I said. "But if you see anybody wandering around or in the house, call the Chief and get back down here."

"Will do," she said, then called over her shoulder. "Unless the dogs are in danger."

"Who the heck would come here in the middle of the night to steal the Tibetan?" Jill said.

"I could probably ballpark it," I said with a dark stare.

"Rooster's cousin?" Sammy said. "He's still hanging around?"

"That's the word on the street," I said. "Let's check the surveillance cameras."

We headed for my office, and I turned on the large flat screen that hung on one of the walls. I grabbed the remote and activated the feed. Four different images appeared in quarters on the screen.

"How the heck do I make this thing go back?" I snapped.

"Hang on," Sammy said, taking the remote from me. "I think it's this one."

"I'm really not in the mood to watch SportsCenter, Sammy," I said, frowning at him.

"Sorry," he said, pressing a different button. "Here we go."

Josie entered the office and sat down on the couch.

"The dogs are fine," she said. "Nobody's been near the house."

"He only wanted the Tibetan," I said.

"Coke Bottle?" Josie said.

"We're gonna find out in a sec," I said, glancing at Sammy.

"Here it is," Sammy said, sitting on the edge of the desk. "This is about two minutes before our phones went off."

We watched the screen in silence then a message started flashing on all four images that the security system had been turned off. Moments later, a figure emerged from the shadows, and we all shook our heads.

"If nothing else, he's predictable," Josie said, staring at Rooster's cousin as he picked the lock on the door leading into the condo area.

214

"And tenacious," I said, folding my arms over my belly as I watched the action play out. "How about that? He got his glasses back."

"Bite him, Wilbur," Josie said without taking her eyes off the screen.

"He's feeding him," I said, staring at the monitor. "And the dog recognizes him."

"Why run the risk of stealing the dog again?" Jill said.

"That dog is incredibly rare and worth a small fortune," Josie said.

"Maybe Coke Bottle isn't happy with his cut from the other thing," I said.

"What other thing?" Sammy said.

"Nothing," I said, waving it off. "I'm just blabbering."

We watched as Coke Bottle attached a lead to the Tibetan and slowly led him out of the Inn. On another camera image, we saw him put the dog in the back seat of a car then drive off.

"Do you recognize the car?" I said to Josie.

"No," she said, exhaling loudly. "Now what?"

"We go get the dog back," I said, heading for the door. Before leaving, I paused and looked at Sammy and Jill. "Do you guys mind sticking around for a while?"

"Sure," Sammy said. "No problem. Where are you going?"

"I just told you. To get the dog."

"You know where it is?" Jill said.

"I've got a pretty good idea."

"I'll call the guy who installed the security system and see when he can get here," Sammy said.

"Tell him if he gets it done tonight, I'll make it worth his while," I said, then nodded at Josie. "You ready?"

"Hang on," she said, heading for her office. "I need to grab something."

I nodded and leaned against the wall as I waited. Then an idea bubbled to the surface, and I headed for a supply closet and grabbed a duffel bag. Josie returned carrying her medical bag and nodded at the duffel I was holding.

"What's that?" she said as we headed outside to the car.

"The parabolic microphones," I said.

"To help us find the dog on your mom's island?"

"Sure," I said, starting the SUV. "Let's go with that."

"You want me to call the Chief?"

I gave it some thought, then shook my head.

"No," I said. "Let's not."

"Because?" she said, raising an eyebrow at me.

"He'll freak out about the possibility of us screwing up his sting operation," I said. "For now, let's see if we can handle this on the QT."

"He's gonna be pissed."

"Nothing gets past you."

"I'm serious, Suzy," she said.

"So am I," I said, pulling into the parking lot behind the restaurant. "I'll be right back."

"You going to give Chef Claire an update?"

"Yeah," I said, about to close the door when I paused. "And pick up a snack."

"Now you sound like me," Josie said.

"Not for us. For Wilbur. You brought lots of sedatives, right?"

"I did. And I've got the tranquilizer gun."

"We won't need to shoot him," I said.

"Because?"

"Because we're bringing him a snack."

"Got it," she said, nodding.

"Do you think Wilbur would prefer steak or chicken?"

"Let's go with beef."

"Good call. Filet Mignon, it is."

I headed inside and gave Chef Claire a quick update as I grabbed two steaks from the walk-in. I listened patiently as she voiced her concerns about our being out on the River in the middle of the night chasing down Rooster's cousin and a two-hundred-pound dog. When she finished, I maintained eye contact with a blank stare on my face.

"Are you listening to me, Suzy?"

"Sure, sure."

"The two of you can't go out there by yourself."

"We're not going by ourselves."

"You're calling Chief Abrams, right?"

"No. Rooster."

217

"Geez, Suzy," Chef Claire said. "You just said you were worried about blowing the investigation. If Rooster gets his hands on his cousin, he's gonna kill him."

"Not if he doesn't leave the boat," I said, flashing a grin at her.

"You've got it all worked out, huh?" Chef Claire said, glaring at me with her hands on her hips.

"Actually, it's sort of a work in progress," I said as I headed out the back door.

"Call me," she shouted from the doorway.

I gave her an over the shoulder finger wave then got back in the car. I tossed the steaks to Josie and grabbed my phone.

"Hey. It's pretty late for you to be calling. What's up?"

I gave Rooster a quick update then waited for his response.

"Where are you?" he said.

"Just leaving the restaurant," I said.

"Head over here. We'll take my boat. Meet me at the dock."

"Thanks, Rooster."

"Hey, you're doing me a favor."

"You can't hurt him tonight, Rooster," I said, my voice rising. "You're going to have to wait a couple of days."

"Maybe."

Chapter 23

I hunkered down to protect myself from the wind as Rooster maintained a steady speed in the direction of Serenity Island.

"You sure you don't want to rethink the Cayman thing?" Josie said, her teeth chattering.

"The thought has crossed my mind," I yelled above the roar of the engine.

Twenty minutes later, Rooster pulled the throttle back as we approached the shallow water on the back side of the island. When he was sure we were out of the pull of the current, he turned the engine off. The boat continued to rock in the breeze, but I was a lot warmer than I'd been on the ride over.

"How far do you think we are from shore?" I said, grabbing the more powerful of the listening devices.

"About fifty yards," Rooster said as he grabbed a pair of high-tech goggles and handed them to Josie. Then he grabbed two more and gave me one before sliding his goggles over his head. I passed out earpieces to both of them then inserted my own into my left ear. I adjusted the volume and nodded when I was happy with it.

"Holy crap, Rooster," Josie said. "Where the heck did you get these things?"

"Amazon," he said, deflecting the question with a casual shrug.

"No way you got these on Amazon," Josie said.

"You're right. I didn't. They're Gen 3, military grade. You can use them as binoculars or wear them as goggles. Pretty cool, huh?"

"Aren't these restricted to only police or military personnel?" I said.

"What's your point?" Rooster said, then laughed. "Hey, you've got your toys, I've got mine."

"Oh, I so need a pair of these," I said, amazed by the clarity of what I was looking at.

"Let me know when you're ready," he said. "I'll give my guy a call."

"Any sign of the dog?" Josie said, slowly turning her head as she scanned the island.

"Not yet," I said. "But somebody is definitely inside the house," I said, adjusting the volume on the microphone. "I can hear the television."

"Your mom's got cable?" Josie said with a frown.

"No, she switched to internet TV last summer," I said. "She says the wireless can be a bit spotty at times, but she loves it."

"She gets everything," Rooster said. "Over a thousand channels. And all the movies even before they leave the theatres."

"How the heck did she manage that?" I said.

"I called my guy," Rooster said with a shrug as he scanned the island. "There he is."

"Coke Bottle?" I said.

"No, the dog. He's sniffing around the shoreline right in front of us. We're upwind from him. He's probably picked up our scent."

"How should we handle this?" I said.

"I'll cut the steaks up into bite-sized pieces. After he eats a couple, I'll start stuffing them with the sedative," Josie said.

"We've got to get closer," Rooster said, grabbing a paddle.

"You're not actually considering getting on shore, are you?" I said.

"Are you out of your mind?" Rooster said, slowly dragging the paddle through the water. "I just want to get close enough to throw them."

"Good call," I said, then turned to Josie. "How long before it starts working?"

"Given his size, I'm gonna guess about an hour," she said, grabbing a scalpel from her bag and quickly cutting the steaks into chunks.

"You should have been a surgeon," Rooster said, admiring her work.

"I am a surgeon," she said, glancing up briefly.

"Yeah, I suppose you are," he said, setting the paddle down on the seat. "Sorry about that."

221

"No worries," she said, handing a couple of the chunks to him.

Rooster removed the goggles then fired one of the pieces in the general direction of the dog.

"How was that?" he said.

"Nice shot," I said. "It landed right next to him. He's sniffing...he's looking around. Bingo."

"I think he likes it," Josie said. "Toss him another one."

Rooster threw another chunk of meat, and the dog quickly tracked it down and devoured it. Now, the Tibetan was officially on the prowl for more.

"Okay, Wilbur. It's time for a nap," Josie said, handing Rooster several pieces of filet loaded with sedatives.

I watched the scene play out through the goggles. The dog devoured every morsel then looked around for more.

"Now we wait," Josie said, leaning back in her seat and grabbing a bag of bite-sized from her coat.

I waved the bag away, then changed my mind and took one. As I chewed, I spotted the front door open, and Coke Bottle stepped out onto the porch.

"I can't believe how clear he is," I said. "These things are amazing."

"He's just lucky I'm not looking at him through a rifle scope," Rooster said.

"Not tonight, Rooster. We're only here to get the dog back."

"I know," he said. "But it's so tempting."

We heard a phone buzz through our earpieces. Then all three of us fixed our goggles on Coke Bottle who was still standing on the porch.

"Yeah," Coke Bottle said. "Nothing. Just watching a little TV."

He listened to what the person on the other end of the line was saying.

"Okay, it don't matter to me. Going early is fine."

"They're moving the drop-off up on Thursday," I said.

"Makes sense," Rooster said. "They're predicting snow. What time do you think they'll do it?"

"Maybe around sunset?" I said. "I doubt if they'd try to do it during the day."

"All right," Coke Bottle snapped into the phone. "You don't have to tell me three times. I got it. I'll be ready to go. You know where to find me." He ended the call, let loose with a short burst of expletives then slid his phone into his pocket. He glanced around the dark. "Wilbur. Wilbur. Where the heck are you?"

"That dog isn't going anywhere," Josie said. "Not as long as he thinks there's more steak falling from the sky."

"You got any left?" I said.

"A couple of pieces," Josie said. "But he's eaten enough to put him out."

"That's fine," I said. "Just toss him a couple more pieces without the sedative. We don't want him wandering off."

223

"Or heading back inside the house," Rooster said, firing another chunk of meat.

We sat quietly for the next half-hour watching the dog and listening to an action movie Coke Bottle had on. Eventually, the dog stretched out, and the sound of soft snoring could be heard through our earpieces.

"Okay," Rooster said, grabbing the paddle and working the boat toward shore. When we were close, he lowered himself into the water that was up to his knees. "Man, that gets your attention."

"I can't believe it," Josie said, staring at him as he casually waded through the frigid water. "He's not human."

"Hardy stock," I said, shaking my head as I watched him kneel down and lift the dog into his arms.

"We better give him some room," Josie said, taking a few steps back from the bow.

Rooster waded back to the boat and gently placed the sleeping dog on the cushioned seat. He climbed in, grabbed a couple of blankets and spread them on the deck. Then he lifted the dog again and set him on top of the blankets. Josie wrapped both blankets around the dog and sat down next to him.

"He's okay, right?" I said, staring down at the massive animal.

"Yeah, he'll be fine. The blankets will keep his core temperature up," she said. "And he'll be out of the wind down there."

"Poor guy," I said. "He's had a tough run of late."

"It'll be over soon," Rooster said. "When is his owner getting back from Hawaii?"

"Friday. He said he'll be driving up as soon as he lands," I said. "Okay, I'm officially freezing my butt off. Let's get out of here."

"Just give me a sec," Rooster said, removing his boots. He dried his bare feet then slipped on a pair of thick socks. "That water is freezing."

"You're actually making a concession to the weather?"

"No, just a general observation."

Chapter 24

I stood in front of the condo watching the Tibetan slowly wake up. Or do his best to do so. The dog yawned then snorted and opened its eyes. He looked around the condo, obviously confused by his surroundings, but then seemed to sigh and dozed off. I headed for the reception area and waited for the coffeemaker to stop gurgling then poured myself a cup.

"You mind pouring me one of those?"

Startled, I flinched and turned to see Josie leaning against the doorjamb.

"You scared the crap out of me," I said, shaking my head as I reached for another mug.

"Sorry," she said, rubbing her eyes. "You're up early."

"Yeah, I couldn't sleep, so I thought I'd come down and check on Wilbur."

"How's he doing?" she said, accepting the mug and taking a sip. "When I left him at three, he was still out."

"He's starting to wake up," I said, heading back into the condo area. We both sat down in chairs in front of the Tibetan's condo and studied the dog as we drank our coffee. "He is a gorgeous dog."

"It's driving you crazy, isn't it?" Josie said, grinning at me.

"What is?"

"The fact that you haven't been able to win him over."

"Maybe a little," I said. "But I've got two days before his owner picks him up. He'll come around."

Josie laughed and the Tibetan stirred. He opened his eyes and stared at both of us. Then he yawned and dropped his head on his front paws as he maintained eye contact.

"Well, at least he's not growling at you," Josie said. "I suppose that's a start. What's that in your hand?"

I held up a small plastic bag.

"I knew I smelled bacon," she said.

"That's probably what woke you up," I said, getting up and slowly approaching the front of the condo. "Good morning, Wilbur. Are you hungry?"

"You're bribing him with bacon? That's cheating."

"Desperate times call for desperate measures," I said, holding a piece of bacon close to the door.

The dog sniffed the air, then slowly got to his feet and took a few steps forward. He glanced back and forth between me and the bacon then sat down on his haunches. I tossed the strip of bacon into the condo, and the Tibetan sniffed then devoured it. He sat back down and looked at me, ready for more.

"You're off to a good start," Josie said. "He's still not snarling."

"Hey, if Coke Bottle figured out a way to handle him, I should be able to, right?"

"I suppose," she said. It was her turn to sniff the air. "Hang on." She grabbed a strand of my hair and held it to her nose. "You changed your shampoo."

"Yeah, I figured Wilbur has associated my scent with our encounter in the storage shed at Jackson's place."

"Unbelievable," Josie said, shaking her head.

"Hey, Wilbur's not the only one who's tenacious," I said, tossing another strip of bacon to the dog. "How's your schedule today?"

"Totally open. And since tomorrow is going to be a marathon, my plan is to keep it that way."

"Good idea," I said, glancing around the condo area. "I think we should paint out here."

"Yeah, that would be a good winter project," Josie said. "But there's no way you're getting on a ladder."

"I'm pregnant, not disabled."

"You're not getting on a ladder," Josie said firmly. "End of story."

"Or what?"

"Or I'll have Chef Claire get her bat."

"Harsh," I said, laughing as I tossed another piece of bacon to the Tibetan who was now drooling. "Good stuff, huh, Wilbur?"

I watched the dog devour it then drifted off, deep in thought.

"What's the matter?" Josie said.

"I was just thinking about Coke Bottle's phone call last night."

"What about it?"

"About them moving the drop-off to an earlier time," I said, frowning.

"They're probably concerned about the possibility of a foot of snow," Josie said. "It makes sense they'd move it up."

"I guess," I said. "But would they try to do it before dark?"

"If it's snowing hard, who's gonna see them out there? Besides, everyone within a hundred miles is going to be watching football or drifting off into a tryptophan coma."

"You know that's a myth, right?"

"About turkey making you sleepy?"

"Yeah," I said. "Other poultry has more tryptophan than turkey. When's the last time you ate fried chicken and needed a nap after?"

"Not a fair question," she said, grinning at me. "I always want a nap after I eat."

"Yeah, I forgot who I was talking to," I said, gently punching her on the shoulder. "It's all the carbs combined with the turkey that makes you sleepy."

"Well, whatever it is," she said. "I'm not going to mess with the formula. I love my afternoon Thanksgiving nap. Not that I'm going to get one tomorrow."

"I don't like our chances," I said. "What time are they planning to do the run? It's driving me nuts."

"Yes, I can see that. You should just let it marinate for a while."

"I suppose you're right," I said, tossing the final piece of bacon to the Tibetan. "But it's bugging me."

The other dogs began stirring, and Josie got to her feet.

"I'm going to let them out to take care of business," she said, heading for the panel that controlled the condo doors leading outside to the play area.

"Let's keep Wilbur in until they've all finished," I said. "He doesn't need any excitement this morning."

"Good call," she said, punching a number into the control panel.

Moments later, all the outside exits opened, except for Wilbur's, and the dogs began shuffling outside. I felt a blast of cold air and shivered. The Tibetan continued to stare at me with an expectant look on his face.

"Sorry, Wilbur. I'm all out of bacon."

The dog snorted and inched closer to the door. I slowly extended my hand toward the dog then pulled it back when the Tibetan let loose with a guttural growl.

"Ingrate," I said, then laughed. "Wilbur, do not bite the hand that feeds you."

"You really thought you could turn him around with a few pieces of bacon?"

"Hey, it always works on you."

"Funny," she said, then spotted Sammy entering the condo area from registration. "Good morning."

"Morning. You guys are up early," he said, studying the Tibetan. "How's he doing?"

"He's fine," Josie said. "But Suzy's feelings are hurt."

"Can't win them all," Sammy said, glancing around. "When did you let them out?"

"Just a couple of minutes ago," Josie said.

"Okay," Sammy said. "Let's give them a few more minutes while I get their breakfast ready."

"Sounds good," Josie said, staring after him as he headed off. "How did we get so lucky?"

"Yeah, he's great," I said. "He's talking about applying to vet school."

"He told me," Josie said. "Not to blow my own horn, but it's really hard to get in."

"I know. But I told him, if he did get in, I'd pay for it."

"You, my friend, are something else," she said, giving me a hug.

"It's the least I can do," I said, then heard my phone buzz. I checked the number then looked at Josie. "I should take this."

"I'm going to grab another cup of coffee. You want one?"

"No, I'm good, thanks." I answered the call. "Good morning, Bill."

"Good morning. I hope I'm not calling too early."

"No, I've been up for a while. I'm trying to do some behavior modification."

"Doing a little self-improvement program?"

"It's too late for that," I said, rubbing my forehead as my neurons turned relentless.

"I just wanted to let you know Shirley and I would like to come to the five o'clock seating tomorrow."

"The last one? I admire your restraint, Detective."

"It's not by choice," he said. "But it's snowing like crazy up here, and the forecast is for a lot more."

"And it's heading our way," I said, shaking my head at the prospect of a white Thanksgiving.

"That's what they're saying," he said. "Anyway, the roads should be cleaned up by tomorrow afternoon. Neither one of us can stand the thought of driving through a mess like that if we don't have to."

"Makes sense," I said. "Don't worry, there's plenty of food."

"That's what I wanted to hear," he said. "Hey, I talked with Shirley last night about that other thing."

"The burglary ring?"

"Yeah. She touched base with all her colleagues and checked the blotter. There haven't been any arrests for burglary matching the description you gave me. You sure your friend got it right?"

My neurons exploded. I sat down and massaged my forehead as I pondered the possibilities and implications of each.

"Are you still there?" he said eventually.

"Sorry. Yeah, I'm here. Is she sure about that?"

"Well, since Shirley is leading the task force, I'd be pretty surprised if she got it wrong."

"I can't argue with your logic."

"Are you okay?"

"I'm fine. Just a little tired. Okay, Bill, we'll see you guys tomorrow afternoon."

"As long as we can make it in, you certainly will."

"Drive safe."

I put my phone away and stared off into the distance. Josie returned with her fresh cup of coffee. She immediately noticed the look on my face and sat down next to me.

"Bad news?" she said, obviously concerned.

"Yeah."

"Gut-punch bad?"

"At a minimum."

Chapter 25

Josie and I got settled in my office while we waited for our guests to arrive. Chloe gave up trying to get comfortable on my lap and hopped up on the desk and rolled over for a tummy rub. Captain was spread across Josie's lap and dominating the couch.

"I can't believe it," Josie said as she gently stroked the Newfie's head.

"The whole thing sucks," I said with a mixture of anger and sadness.

We heard the knock and I invited them in. Chief Abrams and Agent Tompkins entered, and I gestured for them to take a seat on the other side of the desk.

"Man, it is really coming down out there," the Chief said, taking off his coat. "We might be looking at a foot, maybe more."

"Sorry to make you drive over in this weather," I said. "Coffee?"

They both waved my offer off.

"This better be important, Suzy," Agent Tompkins said, glancing at his watch. "I've got a lot on my plate today."

"More than you realize," I said.

"What?"

"Hold your horses. I'll get there."

"What's going on, Suzy?" the Chief said, puzzled.

"I suppose we should start with last night, huh?" I said to Josie.

"Yeah, if we're going to get yelled at, we should probably get it out of the way first," she said.

I nodded then focused on the two cops.

"We had a break-in here last night."

"Someone broke in?" the Chief said.

"Nothing gets past you, Chief."

"Don't start, Josie," he said, glaring at her. He focused on me. "What happened?"

"Coke Bottle came back and stole the Tibetan," I said.

"What?" Agent Tompkins said. "Why the hell would he do that?"

"That dog is worth a fortune," I said with a shrug. "Especially for breeding purposes."

"What an idiot," the Chief said. "How did he get in?"

"He disabled the security system and picked the lock on the back door," I said. "What he didn't know was that we get notified every time the system gets turned on or off. We also have him on video."

"Good," the Chief said. "That will come in handy at his trial for grand theft."

Agent Tompkins snorted.

"You got something to say?" the Chief snapped.

"Dognapping?" the FBI agent said. "I think we can do a lot better than that, Chief. But if you're worried about the dog, we'll see what we can do tomorrow night about getting him back."

I looked at Josie who nodded for me to continue.

"You won't need to worry about that, Agent Tompkins," I said softly.

"Why not?"

"Because the dog is out back resting comfortably."

Agent Tompkins scowled as he thought about my comment. Chief Abrams cocked his head at me.

"What did you do, Suzy?" the Chief said.

"We rescued the dog last night," I said, going for casual.

"You did what?" Agent Tompkins said.

"We drove over to Serenity Island and rescued the dog. Actually, it was a lot easier than we thought it would be."

"Piece of cake," Josie said.

"Why on earth would you do that?" the Chief said.

"Rhetorical, right?"

"Josie, I'm warning you," he said, glaring at her again before fixing a hard stare on me. "Why?"

"Because nobody steals one of our dogs. Especially that moron."

Exasperated, the Chief ran a hand through his hair and looked at his colleague.

"Did you give any thought to the possibility of how badly you could have jeopardized my investigation?" Agent Tompkins said. "Or already have?"

"Actually, we did," I said, nodding.

"And?" the FBI agent said, leaning forward in his chair.

"We went anyway."

"You went anyway," Agent Tompkins said with a blank stare.

"Did Walter see you?" the Chief said.

"He did not," I said.

"Are you sure?"

"Positive," Josie said.

"Just the two of you went?" Agent Tompkins said.

"No, Rooster was with us," I said. "Somebody had to carry the dog."

"You never stop, do you?" Agent Tompkins said.

"Are you kidding?" the Chief said. "She's been on her best behavior this week."

"Thank you, Chief," I said, beaming at him.

"How can you be sure he didn't see you?" the Chief said.

"We had night vision goggles on him," Josie said.

"Rooster's new toy, right?" the Chief said.

"How did you know?" I said.

"He showed them to me a couple of weeks ago," he said. "I just ordered a pair."

"They're incredible, huh?"

"Amazing technology."

"Can we please get back to the topic at hand?" the FBI agent said to no one in particular.

"Whatever you say, Agent Tompkins," I said, forcing a smile. "After all, it is *your* investigation."

He flinched but remained silent. Eventually, he nodded and looked at the Chief.

"Well, as long as they weren't seen, we should be fine. No harm, no foul, right?"

"Yeah," the Chief said, not taking his eyes off me.

"Thanks for letting us know," Agent Tompkins said, standing up. "And I'm glad to hear the dog is safe and sound."

"Hang on," the Chief said, holding a hand up as he maintained his stare.

"C'mon, Chief. Let's go. We're already behind schedule."

"You're not done, are you?" the Chief said.

"No. There's more," I said.

"Why am I not surprised?" Agent Tompkins said, sitting back down. "She's got more. What did you do? Put floating IED's around your mother's dock?"

"Funny," I said, returning the agent's stare. "While we were there last night, Walter got a phone call."

"I suppose you saw him through your night vision goggles," Agent Tompkins said.

"We did. But we also heard him," I said.

"Your new parabolic mic, right?" the Chief said.

238

"Yup. And you wouldn't believe how well the sound travels over water," I said.

"Okay, I'll play," an agitated Agent Tompkins said. "What did he say on the call?"

"He was listening primarily," I said. "You know, being told what to do." I looked back and forth at both men before continuing. "They're moving the time up."

"Moving it up?" Agent Tompkins said, then looked at the Chief. "That makes sense with the weather. Did they say what time?"

"They did not," I said.

"Okay," the FBI agent said. "We'll be ready to go tomorrow whatever time they decide to make their move. Did he say anything else on the phone?"

"No," I said, shaking my head.

"All right, then," he said, again starting to get up from his chair. "Thanks to both of you. Well done."

"Hang on," the Chief said, again reaching out and placing a hand on Agent Tompkins arm. "There's still more, isn't there?"

"Yeah," I said with a sad smile.

"Of course," the agent said as he settled back into his chair. "She's got even more. What's the deal, Suzy? Are you working on your storytelling abilities, or do you just enjoy busting my stones?"

"Probably a bit of both," I said, managing a small grin.

"Then by all means," he said, spreading his arms wide. "Lay it on us."

"I got a phone call this morning. From a friend of ours who's a detective in Ottawa."

"Okay," Agent Tompkins said. "I'm gonna guess it's connected to what we're doing down here."

"Yeah, unfortunately, it is," I said softly. "We've been talking about how there must be another person involved in the smuggling ring."

"We've been talking about it constantly," the Chief said. "Someone behind the scenes pulling all the strings."

"Yeah. The mastermind."

"And?" Agent Tompkins said.

"And there is," I said, staring at him.

"You got a name?"

I took a deep breath then exhaled loudly.

"Betty," I whispered.

"Betty? That's ridiculous," Agent Tompkins said, then chortled. "You should have quit while you were ahead, Suzy. What the hell is wrong with you? Betty is a decorated FBI agent who's on the fast track."

"I know that," I said. "And Josie and Chef Claire were very impressed with her work in Italy."

"There you go," he said. "That should tell you everything you need to know about Betty."

"I really wish it did," I whispered.

"Me too," Josie said, nodding.

"What's going on, Suzy?" the Chief said.

"Betty's story about her house being robbed is a lie."

"And the cop from Ottawa told you this?" Agent Tompkins said.

"He did."

"So, he's somehow in the loop about the gang robberies up there?"

"He is. His wife heads the task force that's working on it," I said.

Agent Tompkins flinched and sat back in his chair, deep in thought.

"And there's no record of her house being robbed," I said. "Her story about being in Ottawa the other day is a big, fat lie. And so is her need to go back today to meet with the police."

"I don't believe it," Agent Tompkins said.

"Has Betty ever been assigned to the southern border? California? Maybe Texas?" I said to Agent Tompkins.

"She spent some time in Texas. Near Brownsville. She transferred back home to Ottawa a couple of years ago."

"Brownsville's a border town, right?" I said.

"It is," Agent Tompkins said.

"Where did Joshua Williams say he was relocating from?" I said to the Chief.

"Harlingen," he said. "I have no idea where it is."

241

"It's about half an hour from Brownsville," Agent Tompkins said, frowning. "No, I refuse to believe it. Not Betty. Anybody but Betty."

"She's been coming to the restaurant about once a month since last spring," Josie said.

"Sure. She's been working the investigation," Agent Tompkins said.

"Or she was in town every time the runs were taking place," I said.

"Geez," the Chief said. "What a perfect cover."

"Yes, it certainly is," I said. "So, when things started to heat up on the southern border, she decides it's time to transfer back home and approach human trafficking differently. What reason did she use to justify her request for the transfer?"

"Sick mother," Agent Tompkins said softly.

"Did you ever check her story out?" the Chief said.

"Why would I do that?" Agent Tompkins said, staring at the Chief.

"Sure, I get that," the Chief said, nodding. "You guys have been working together for a long time."

"I trust Betty with my life." Agent Tompkins said, then stared down at the floor. "At least I did."

"How many times has Betty been to your office, Chief?" I said.

"She's been there a bunch of times. Mostly just to stop by and say hello when she was in town. Why?"

"I'm wondering how she figured out where you kept the spare keys."

"You think she was the one who helped Walter escape?" Agent Tompkins said.

"I do," I said. "She was in the boathouse when you guys grabbed Coke Bottle, and we got the dog back. Then she left to return the boat, and we all met at the restaurant an hour or so later."

"She could have slipped inside after we headed to C's," the Chief said, then corrected himself. "No, she would have waited until she set off Jackson's alarm and George left the station."

"Yeah, she didn't worry about Coke Bottle until after," I said.

"After what?" the Chief said.

"After she shot Roger Smith."

"Geez," the Chief grunted. "She had plenty of time to get to the island and back in time to meet us."

"She certainly did," I whispered.

"And she was the one who cut Coke Bottle out of the duct tape," Josie said. "She must have followed us to the island."

"Coke Bottle probably texted her from the van," I said. "It was the same night she said she was in Ottawa because of the break-in."

"She volunteered to return Walter's glasses," Agent Tompkins said, shaking his head.

"And she also blamed you for the screw up with the fake IDs," I said.

"I knew she didn't say anything to me about keeping track of those documents," Agent Tompkins said. "I've been worried I'm starting to lose it."

"Don't beat yourself up, Agent Tompkins," I said. "She's played this thing beautifully. Apart from her choice of Coke Bottle to help her."

"She's gotta be furious with Walter," the Chief said.

"My guess is she considers him a loose end," I said.

"Yeah," Agent Tompkins said softly as he stared out the window. "Betty. I still can't believe it."

"Why would she kill the guy who was producing the fake IDs?" Josie said.

"Maybe he wasn't happy with his cut," the Chief said. "Greed is always a good motive."

"Or she's going to grab all the money for herself and run," I said. "If she was bringing people across the border from Mexico, combined with what she's been able to get away with here, she's probably stashed away quite a nest egg. This run alone is going to be worth a couple million."

"Betty could resign from the Bureau and walk away to spend the rest of her life with her toes in the sand," Agent Tompkins said. "With her reputation, nobody would ever suspect her of anything."

"It's pretty close to the perfect crime," Chief Abrams said. "I'm impressed."

"Me too," I said. "There's just one problem."

"What's that?" Agent Tompkins said.

"She got caught," I said with a shrug.

"Yeah, there is that," Agent Tompkins said, nodding. "Okay, I need to run and make a few phone calls. My game plan is going to need some adjustments." Then he caught the look on my face. "What is it now?"

"I'd let the whole thing play itself out," I said. "But that's just me. It's *your* investigation."

"You really need to learn how to win gracefully, Suzy," Agent Tompkins said, his anger again flaring.

"Nobody's won anything yet," I said.

"Well, if you come up with any ideas about how to handle Thursday, you be sure to let me know."

"I don't think I like your attitude, Agent Tompkins."

"Think?" Josie said, glaring at the FBI agent. "There's no doubt as far as I'm concerned."

"Thank you," I said, beaming at her before focusing on the Fed. "I'm afraid the only thought I have about Thursday is how much gravy to put on my turkey."

"You're gonna quit now?" Agent Tompkins said, his tone bordering on mocking.

"I wouldn't think of it," I said, giving him a crocodile smile.

245

"Okay, before this conversation ends badly, I need to make some calls."

Agent Tompkins again started to get up out of his chair. The Chief, studying me closely, again held out a hand to stop him.

"Hang on," the Chief said.

"Again? Now what?"

"Why the Thursday gravy reference?"

"Because they're doing the run tonight," I said, gently running my nails over Chloe's belly.

"Tonight?" the Chief said, frowning.

"Of course. Why else would Betty say she needed to go Ottawa today?"

Chapter 26

Two hours later, I was savoring a bowl of chili when I caught the look Chief Abrams was giving me.

"Did I spill?" I said, giving myself a quick once-over.

"No," he said, then took a big bite of his sandwich. He continued to study my face as he chewed. "I don't see a trace of chili on you. Well done."

"Then what's up with the frowny face?"

"It's just that some days I feel like I should be giving you half my salary. How the heck did you piece all this together?"

"I've had this nagging thought someone in an official capacity had to be involved," I said with a shrug. "At first, I thought it might be the woman from Fish and Wildlife, but that didn't work for me. But when I talked with the detective in Ottawa, something clicked. I just worked backward from there."

"I can't believe Betty could do something like this," Chef Claire said. "After our time with her in Italy, I was convinced she was a rock star. You know, one of the good guys who's looking out for us."

"It's sad," Josie said, sliding her empty bowl aside.

"I wonder how she and my cousin got connected," Rooster said.

"She must have put the word out they were looking for somebody who knew their way around the River," I said.

"And it had to be somebody who didn't mind getting his hands dirty," the Chief said.

"You think Betty plans on taking Coke Bottle out tonight?" Josie said.

"I'm hoping she leaves that to me," Rooster said, then caught the looks we were giving him. "I'm joking. Death is too good for Walter. He needs to be locked up for several years in a confined space. Hopefully, without his glasses."

"I think she might try," I said. "Loose ends and all that."

"Joshua Williams, too?" Josie said.

"Maybe," I said with a shrug. "Unless their relationship extends past a business partnership."

"Now, there's a thought," Josie said. "They take out Coke Bottle then slip away into the mist with millions."

"I don't know about the mist," I said. "From the looks of things, it'll be more like a blizzard."

Agent Tompkins approached the table, frowned when he saw me, but sat down next to the Chief and beamed at Chef Claire.

"I was hoping we could talk alone," he said to the Chief.

"Everybody here knows what's going on, Agent Tompkins," Chief Abrams said.

248

"Yeah, I suppose you're right," he said, sounding defeated. "The hell with it." He glanced around the table. "How's the chili?"

"Excellent," Josie said.

"Can I bring you a bowl?" Chef Claire said, smiling at him.

"That would be great. Thanks."

Chef Claire got up from the table and headed for the kitchen.

"Did you talk to Betty?" the Chief said.

"I did. Said she was heading to Ottawa early because of the weather."

"What did your boss in Washington have to say?" the Chief said.

"He was devastated by the news about her. But he said we should just let it play out," he said, nodding in my direction. "You missed your calling."

"Thanks, but I'll pass," I said, then slid a spoonful of chili into my mouth.

"But I'm afraid we have a problem," Agent Tompkins said.

"You mean apart from having a corrupt agent inside your tent?" Josie said.

"Yeah, apart from that," he said, rubbing his forehead with both hands. "Nobody is going to be able to get in because of the weather."

"That's not good," Chief Abrams said.

"I just got off the phone with the FBI office in Buffalo. They've got a foot and a half already. Whiteout conditions all over the city. It sounds like everyone was caught off guard by the storm."

"And it's a holiday," the Chief said.

"Yeah, everybody I called is working with skeleton crews."

"Everyone is hunkered down for family, food, and football," Josie said.

"Did you talk to the state police?" the Chief said.

"Same deal. Skeleton crews and most of them are out dealing with the storm. There's already been a bunch of car accidents."

"What about the Coast Guard?" I said.

"They can provide two guys and one boat."

"I could make some calls to nearby towns," the Chief said. "But I don't like our chances. They're small forces. I imagine they're down to one cop trying to keep an eye on things."

"Can you fly some extra people in?" Josie said.

"There's not enough time," Agent Tompkins said. "And they probably can't fly in this storm anyway. Is your deputy around?"

"George? No, he's spending Thanksgiving with family out on the west coast."

"How about Jackson?" Agent Tompkins said. "You said he used to have your job."

"Now, there's an idea," the Chief said. "He knows the River really well. If he can make it, we'll be able to add an extra boat. He can drive you."

"That would make three," Agent Tompkins said. "It's still not enough."

"What do you need?" Rooster said.

"Extra eyes for surveillance primarily," Agent Tompkins said. "Given the snowstorm, even if Jackson can do it, three boats aren't enough to monitor the island."

"And it would be pretty easy to slip away," the Chief said. "Especially if they pick the right dock."

"The right dock?" Josie said.

"There's four on the island," I said.

"I did not know that," Josie said, then frowned. "This is probably a dumb question, but why does your mom need four docks?"

"She hates docking her boat in the wind," I said.

Rooster nodded in agreement.

"She had a bad experience several years ago," he said. "The wind pushed her boat onto the rocks, and it scared the crap out of her."

"Now she uses whichever dock is most protected from the wind," I said.

Chef Claire returned carrying a steaming bowl of chili and placed it in front of Agent Tompkins. She sat back down and resumed work on her salad.

"Thanks, Chef Claire. It's delicious."

"You're very welcome."

Josie and I grinned at each other as we watched the flirtation play itself out.

"What did I miss?" Chef Claire said.

"We were just talking about not having enough people to handle tonight," the Chief said.

"You want some help?" she said.

"No, you have more important things to do," Josie said.

"Like what?"

"Like cooking for three hundred," Josie said, then laughed.

"Yeah, there is that," Chef Claire said.

"But I'm free," I said, tossing it out.

"No," Chief Abrams said. "Absolutely not."

"Why not?" I said, already protesting. "We were out there last night. And that was without any cops tagging along."

"Tagging along?" Agent Tompkins said.

"Figure of speech," I said, waving it off.

"On a night when no one was carrying guns," the Chief said. "No way in hell, Suzy."

"Fine," I said, miffed. "Go right ahead and let a smuggling ring slip away. I'm sure the Bureau will be delighted with Agent Tompkins' performance."

"Don't start," the Chief said, one eyebrow going up.

"Let's hear her out, Chief," Agent Tompkins said.

"Thank you," I said, beaming at him.

"Don't thank me yet. At the moment, I'm just listening."

"You'll need at least four boats to cover the island," I said. "And between Rooster and me, we have everything we need to keep a close eye on our assigned area. Don't we, Rooster?"

"I'm really not comfortable with this conversation, Suzy," he said, shaking his head. "Do you have any idea what your mother would do if she heard her pregnant daughter was out on the River helping the cops? At night? In this weather?"

"I could probably ballpark it."

"Suzy," Rooster said, his voice rising in warning.

"Don't worry. I'll handle my mother."

"You're going to tell her?" Rooster said.

"Absolutely."

"When?"

"Probably sometime tomorrow," I said softly, then glanced around the table.

"Geez, this is gonna be a problem," Josie said. "Not a good idea, Suzy."

"Going out on the River tonight, or waiting until tomorrow to tell my mom?"

"Take your pick."

"Come on, lighten up, guys," I said. "We're just going to be sitting in Rooster's boat watching. It's not like we're going to get caught in the crossfire."

"Oh, I've got such a bad feeling about this," the Chief said.

"Which of the four docks is least likely to be used tonight?" Agent Tompkins said.

"The one at the main boathouse," Rooster and I said in unison. We both laughed, and I motioned for him to explain.

"The main boathouse has northern exposure," he said. "And that's the direction the storm is coming from. It'll be hard to get in and out of there tonight. Especially if you're worried about the safety of the people you've got on the boat."

"Exactly," I said. "So, you assign us that one. That way, you won't have to worry about watching it."

"And if they decide to use that dock for some reason?" the Chief said.

"We'll give you a call on the radio and quietly slip away," I said, then looked at Rooster. "What do you think?"

"I think you've completely lost your mind," he said. "She's going to go crazy, Suzy."

"What he said," Josie said. "This is such a bad idea."

"I suppose I could go by myself," I said, playing my trump card.

Rooster and Josie stared at each other for a long time.

"Suzy, please," Josie said softly. "Think of the baby."

"The baby is and will be, just fine," I snapped. "We're just going for a late season boat ride to watch and listen to a conversation."

"Unbelievable," Josie said as she glared at me. "And I thought the Tibetan was tenacious."

"I'm not being stubborn. I'm merely offering my services to help out a couple of my favorite and incredibly dedicated LEOs."

"LEOs?" Chef Claire said.

"Law enforcement officers," the Chief said. "Has she been binging on cop shows again?"

"Season four of Bosch," I said, glancing over at him. "It's great."

"I'm still trying to finish up season three," the Chief said.

Agent Tompkins cleared his throat loudly.

"Sorry," I said. "So, what do you say?"

"I say no," Rooster said.

"I say we lock you in the closet the rest of the night," Josie said.

"You'll have to catch me first."

"Yeah, like that's going to be a problem," she said, laughing.

"Okay, that's it. I'm gonna tell your mother," Rooster said, his voice rising.

"You wouldn't dare," I said, glaring at him.

"Watch me," he said, grabbing his phone from his pocket and leaving the table.

"I can't believe he's doing that," I said, stunned.

"If he didn't call her, I would have," Josie said.

Five minutes later, Rooster sat back down at the table with a smug look I so wanted to knock off. I avoided eye contact with him as I finished my bowl of chili. I was perusing the dessert menu when my mother strolled up and sat down across from me. She said quiet hellos to everyone then fixed a hard stare on me.

"Rooster said you have something to tell me."

"He's the one who felt the need to share," I said, finally making eye contact with him. "You're on, Big Mouth."

Rooster was about to respond, then thought better of it. He turned to my mother and began telling her the story. I kept a close eye on my mother for signs she was nearing the boiling point, but she listened closely, occasionally nodding. When Rooster finished, she took a sip from the glass of wine Chef Claire had insisted she was going to need, then sat back and exhaled loudly.

"Well, this is one for the scrapbook," she said. "Or perhaps scrapheap might be a better term."

"It's not a big deal, Mom," I whispered.

"Where do I even begin?" she said, then focused on the Chief. "Is Rooster's story about tonight accurate?"

"It is," Chief Abrams said, also keeping a close eye on her.

"Do you really need a fourth boat?" she said, turning to Agent Tompkins.

"If I'm being honest, it would help."

"Then, by all means, you should have a fourth boat," she said. "This smuggling ring is despicable."

"What?" Rooster said.

"Geez, I would have bet you my car she wasn't going to say that," Josie said.

"Thanks, Mom," I said, stunned.

"Hold your horses, young lady," she said, giving me her best crocodile smile. "I said they should have a fourth boat. What I didn't say was that you could be on it."

"Crap."

"Good one, Mrs. C.," Josie said with a grin.

"Thank you, dear," my mother said, nodding back at her. "I thought it was rather good myself."

"C'mon, Mom," I said. "It's no big deal. I know the River like the back of my hand. Even in this weather. And we won't be anywhere near the action. I'll just be there to lend my eyes and ears."

"I'm quite sure Rooster will be able to handle it," she said.

"It's not fair, and you know it."

"Teenage temper tantrum is not your best play at the moment, young lady."

"Well, I'm running low on options," I said, then laughed and reached out to pat her hand. "I understand your concern, Mom. I really do."

"Then problem solved," she said. "You're not going. End of discussion."

"When are you going to start treating me like an adult?"

"Rhetorical, right?" my mother said, then grinned at Josie.

"Well done, Mrs. C. You're on fire today."

"Thank you, dear. Do you really want me to answer that question, darling?"

"Forget it," I said, desperate for a new approach. "If you don't agree to let me go, Mom, I'm going to nag you about it on a daily basis all winter."

She flinched but quickly recovered. But not fast enough.

"That's right, Mom. So, instead of spending the winter talking about all the wonderful things we're going to do with your new granddaughter, you can look forward to a daily harangue about your unwillingness to support me. Especially if the smugglers somehow manage to escape tonight. If that happens, I can't even imagine the amount of guilt I'll be dealing with. Not to mention all the stress."

"Blackmail? You're resorting to blackmail?"

"Blackmail is such a harsh term. Let's call it, *retribution*."

"Why on earth are you so insistent about going?" she said, her voice rising.

"Because I'm the one who figured out what's going on around here, and I'd like to see it through."

My mother was silent for several moments then looked back and forth at the Chief and Agent Tompkins.

"Is she telling the truth?" my mother said. "About being the one who figured all this out?"

Both cops nodded their heads in silence. My mother massaged her forehead with both hands then focused on me.

"I can't believe I gave birth to Sherlock Holmes," she whispered.

"Normally, I'd take that as a compliment, but I don't think that's how you meant it."

"Nice to see you're paying attention, darling," she said, then exhaled audibly. "Okay, you can go. On one condition."

"All right. Now you're talking," I said, perking up. "What is it?"

"That I'm on the boat with you," she said. "Just to make sure you don't do anything stupid."

"You want to tag along?" I said, caught off-guard by her response.

"Want probably isn't the word I would use."

"Funny, Mom. Cool. There's plenty of room on the boat. And Rooster has an extra pair of night vision goggles."

"I can't wait," she said, draining what was left in her wine glass.

"I don't believe it," Rooster said. "She folded. How the hell did she talk her into it?"

"Have you ever been around her when she's on one of her multi-week sulks?" Josie said.

"Can't say that I have."

"Count your blessings," Josie said.

"Hey," I said, making a face at her. "Whose side are you on?"

"Take a wild guess."

"I assume you'll be covering all four docks on the island," my mother said to Agent Tompkins.

"We will."

"Then we'll take the one at the main boathouse," she said. "There's no way anyone in their right mind would try to get a boat in and out of there in this wind."

"We are talking about Walter here," Rooster said.

"You do have a point," my mother said. "One more thing, darling."

"What's that, Mom?"

"After tonight, you're going to promise me there will be no more shenanigans until after the baby is born."

"Of course, Mom. Do I look like a total idiot?"

My mother gnawed on her bottom lip but said nothing.

"Relax, Mom. Just think of the story you'll be able to tell your granddaughter."

"I'll add it to the list."

Chapter 27

We met at Rooster's marina just before four o'clock. The wind was up, and the snow continued to fall at the rate of a couple inches an hour. Well over a foot of fresh snow greeted us when we stepped out of my SUV and slowly made our way to the edge of the dock.

"Hang on a sec," Rooster said, brandishing a shovel. He quickly shoveled the dock that led to a boathouse then walked back to us. "Take your time. It's a bit slippery in spots."

"Shouldn't we wait for my mom?" I said.

"She's already here," he said. "Her car's in the garage."

We slowly made our way along the dock then stepped inside the boathouse. My mother was in the boat arranging a stack of blankets and a couple of boxes. When she heard us, she turned around and put her hands on her hips as she studied my outfit.

"Are you sure you're going to be warm enough, darling?"

"Yeah, I layered up, Mom," I said, nodding at the form-fitting snowmobile suit she was wearing. "Hey, cute outfit. Is that new?"

"It is," she said, striking a pose. "Since we're spending the winter here, I thought it was time for a new one. I've also got it

261

in canary yellow. But I thought black was more appropriate for tonight."

"It's going to look great with your night vision goggles," I deadpanned.

"Don't push your luck, young lady."

Two boats came into view at the edge of the boathouse. They idled next to each other, and the Chief and Jackson waved. Agent Tompkins, looking absolutely miserable, was sitting next to Jackson.

"Are you guys ready?" Chief Abrams said.

"We are," Rooster said. "Where's the Coast Guard boat?"

"They're waiting for us at the entrance to the bay," the Chief said.

"How bad is it out there?" I said.

"It sucks," Jackson said. "Need I go on?"

"No, we got it," I said. "Why are you so grumpy?"

"Williams backed out of the deal today," Jackson said. "The store is officially back on the market."

"I'm sorry, Jackson. Did he give you a reason?" I said.

"He said he needs to head back to Texas."

"Why?"

"His mother's sick."

"Ah, an oldie but a goodie," Josie said.

"What?" Jackson said, confused.

"Nothing. Okay, let's go catch some human traffickers," Josie said, sliding into her seat and draping a blanket over her shoulders.

"I thought we'd do a convoy on the way over," the Chief said. "You mind taking the lead, Rooster? You know the River better than any of us."

"No problem," Rooster said. "We'll run the channel all the way then make a ninety-degree turn just before Picture Island."

"Okay," the Chief said. "Let's get going. It's going to be dark soon."

"How can you tell?" Josie said, wrapping the blanket tight around her.

Rooster dug through a duffel bag and slid a pair of goggles on. He handed my mother and me each a set then cursed under his breath.

"What's the matter?" my mother said.

"I'm missing a set," he said as he continued to rummage through the bag. "I can't believe it."

"Coke Bottle," I said.

"He must have snuck into the boathouse at some point," Rooster said. "Damn it."

"It's okay," Josie said. "I don't need a pair."

"We'll share," I said.

"Don't worry about it," she said, shivering. "Let's just get this over with."

Rooster slowly accelerated out of the boathouse then looked over his shoulder to make sure the other two boats were following.

"These things are amazing," my mother said, glancing around through her goggles.

"Military issue," Rooster said.

"You got them from the guy, right?" my mother said.

"Yeah," he said, pressing the throttle down until the boat planed.

A few minutes later, we spotted the Coast Guard runabout idling. Rooster tapped the horn once, and the boat took up its position at the back of our small convoy. When we reached the deep-water channel, Rooster relaxed a bit and maintained a slow, steady speed. Even with the goggles, visibility was horrible, and the snow continued to fall and swirl in the wind.

"A little different from July, huh?" I said, managing a small laugh through chattering teeth. I glanced over at Josie who had made herself as small as possible. "How are you doing?"

"Ask me in July."

"Oh, I almost forgot," Rooster said, grabbing a walkie-talkie from the duffel bag and turning it on. He fiddled with one of the buttons until he located the right frequency. "Chief, you there?"

"I'm here. How's the clarity?"

"Perfect," Rooster said. "Where did you get these?"

"From Agent Tompkins," the Chief said. "He says it's the only brand the Bureau uses."

"Nice," Rooster said, nodding. "I wouldn't mind a set of these."

"Me either," the Chief said.

"Let me know and I'll call my guy," Rooster said. "Hey, Coast Guard. Can you hear me?"

"Five by five," someone from the runabout replied.

"Jackson. Are you there?" the Chief said.

"I have no idea where I am at the moment, Chief," Jackson said, laughing. "But I can hear you just fine."

"Okay, we're all set," the Chief said. "Agent Tompkins?"

"Yeah?"

"Since Rooster's going to be covering the main boathouse, I thought you and I would cover the southern and western sides of the island. And our Coast Guard friends can keep an eye on the dock at the eastern end. Given the direction of the wind, I'm betting Walter will use one of the two we'll be watching."

"Sounds like a plan, Chief," Agent Tompkins said. "You got a preference?"

"Not really. How about I take the west side?"

"That's fine," the FBI agent said. "Is that okay with you, Jackson?"

"Sure," he said. "I'm familiar with the island."

"Are you guys from the Coast Guard good with covering the east end?"

"Affirmative. How do you want to handle the lights when we get there?"

"Just to be safe," Agent Tompkins said. "I think all the lights on the boats should be off."

"Safe?"

"As in, not being seen," Agent Tompkins said.

"Got it. Okay, but let's hope there aren't any other idiots out here tonight," one of the Coast Guard guys said. "Going to a watery grave in the middle of a blizzard isn't how I planned to spend Thanksgiving."

"There's a cheery thought," Josie said. "Ooh, hot chocolate. Thanks, Mrs. C. You think of everything."

"Would you like a cup, darling?"

"Yes, please."

"Rooster?"

"Sounds good," Rooster said, handing my mother a pint of brandy. "Pour a nice shot of that into it if you wouldn't mind."

"Mind? I think I'll join you," my mother said.

Twenty minutes later, Rooster slowed and made a ninety-degree turn. Soon, he pulled the throttle back to neutral and drifted.

"Okay, we're here," he said into the walkie-talkie.

"We are?" Agent Tompkins said.

"Serenity is a couple hundred yards directly in front of us," Rooster said. "If you look up at the top of the island, you should be able to see some lights."

"Barely," Agent Tompkins said.

"I got this," Jackson said. "So, what's the plan?"

"If you see anything, just get on the radio," Agent Tompkins said. "And again, you need to stay out of the way, Rooster. Just let Chief Abrams and I handle the capture. But if you guys from the Coast Guard think you can help, feel free to join in. Is everybody clear?"

The other boats confirmed their understanding, and Rooster slowly accelerated. When we could make out the shoreline through the goggles, he veered right and continued around to the back of the island. When we were about fifty yards away from the main boathouse, he turned the engine and the lights off and dropped anchor. We sat silently for a few minutes taking in the surreal nature of our surroundings.

"This is really weird," Josie said. "I feel like I'm in the Hunger Games."

"You want to borrow my goggles for a while to get your bearings?" I said.

"No, I'm fine. I'll just sit here in the dark and enjoy my hot chocolate."

I scanned the area around the boathouse.

"You see anything?"

"No, I don't," Rooster said.

"There are definitely lights on up at the house," my mother said. "And I just saw two people walk past the window."

"Did you get a good look at them?" I said, focusing on the house.

"No."

"Do you think Coke Bottle has already left to do the pickup?" I said.

"That would be my guess," Rooster said. "I know I'd want to get it over with as soon as possible."

"I wish I could see the look on those people's faces when they meet Coke Bottle," Josie said, chuckling.

"With a pair of these goggles on, his vision is going to be improved," Rooster said. "Especially if he's smart enough to figure out how to use the magnification feature."

"Does anybody see anything yet?" Agent Tompkins said through the radio.

Everyone responded in the negative then the Chief spoke.

"Is everyone in position?"

"Affirmative."

"Yeah, we're anchored off the boathouse," Rooster said.

"Okay, now we wait," Agent Tompkins said.

Rooster took a sip of his hot chocolate, nodded his approval at my mother, then rummaged through the duffel bag. He removed an odd-looking weapon.

"What the heck is that?" I said.

"It's the next to last option," he said, examining the rifle. He grabbed a pistol from the bag and set it down next to him.

"What's that?"

"The last option," he deadpanned.

"Funny. You brought a rifle?" I said, frowning.

"It's a tranquilizer gun," he said, removing a small satchel from the duffel.

"What do you need with a tranquilizer gun?" I said.

"For my cabin in the Adirondacks," he said, then winced and grabbed his lower back.

"What's the matter?" my mother said.

"This damn cold wreaks havoc on my back," he said, grimacing. "Okay, it's passing."

"Spasm?" my mother said.

"Yeah, I had one this morning that brought me to my knees," he said.

"This is not the place to be when you're dealing with back spasms," my mother said.

"I'll be fine," he said. "Anyway, I always take the gun with me when I go to my cabin."

"Bears, right?" I said.

"Yeah, I quit hunting animals when I was a kid. But after I woke up one morning and found a three-hundred-pound bear on my front porch, I decided I better have something around to protect myself."

"Good call," I said. "What sort of ammo does it shoot?"

"It fires darts loaded with sedatives," he said, handing me the gun. "If I'm lucky, I'll be able to get a shot at my cousin tonight."

269

"Rooster," I said, my voice rising in warning.

"I'm kidding," he said.

"Really?"

"Maybe."

"What's in the sedative?" I said, handing the gun back to him.

"It's a combination of Xylazine and Ketamine," he said. "We did some research about what's recommended to neutralize a bear without hurting it."

"We?" I said, laughing. "Let me guess, you called the guy?"

"No," he said, frowning. "I called Josie."

"You did?"

"I'm a vet," she said. "I have access to stuff like that."

"And you gave it to him?" I said, surprised.

"Would you rather he shoots bears with a hollow point?"

"Fair point," I said, nodding. "Is giving animal sedatives to civilians legal?"

"It depends on who you talk to," Josie said.

"Who did you talk to?"

"Nobody."

Rooster laughed as he opened the satchel. He removed two darts with different colored ends.

"Remind me again. Which one is which?" he said to Josie.

"The blue tip is a full dose for an adult bear. You use the red one if you're dealing with a cub. It's about a third of the adult dose."

"Got it," he said, loading the rifle.

My mother topped off our hot chocolates, and we sipped in silence. Then I noticed a change in the weather.

"Hey, the snow is letting up."

"And the wind is dying," Rooster said. "I think it actually feels a bit warmer.

"Yeah, it's downright balmy," Josie said.

"Shhh," my mother said, cocking her head and concentrating hard. "Do you hear that?"

"It's a boat," Rooster said, scanning the horizon through his goggles. "Holy crap. I don't believe it."

"What is it?" I said, following his stare. "Are you kidding me?"

"What's going on?" Josie said.

"Coke Bottle is driving my mom's party boat," I said, still stunned by what I was seeing.

"The pontoon boat?" Josie said.

"Yeah," my mother said, shaking her head.

"Let me see," Josie said.

I handed her my goggles, and she fiddled with the focus before taking a long look at the bizarre sight. She removed the goggles and handed them back to me.

"How the heck did he manage to steal your party boat, Mrs. C.?" Josie said.

"It was stored at my place," Rooster said. "I was planning on taking it out of the water on Friday."

"Unbelievable," I whispered. "He figured out a way to get them all over here in one trip. That's a boatload of people. Reminds me of the time when we pulled that all-nighter a couple of years ago."

"That was a great party," Josie said.

"What all-nighter?" my mother said, glancing at me.

"Never mind," I said, waving it off. "Long story."

"He's heading straight for the main boathouse," Rooster said.

"And look who's walking down from the house," I said.

"Who is it?" Josie said.

"Betty and Joshua Williams," I said. "Time to get on the radio, Rooster."

"Chief. Agent Tompkins," Rooster said into the walkie-talkie.

"What is it?" the FBI agent said.

"We have visuals on the boat," Rooster said. "They're heading straight for the boathouse on our side."

"Is it loaded with people?" the Chief said.

"It is."

"Should we come around to that side of the island?" someone from the Coast Guard boat said.

"What do you think?" Rooster said, glancing around the boat.

"No, don't do that," I said, reaching out for the radio. "May I?"

"Be my guest," he said, handing it over.

"Can you guys all hear me?" I said into the walkie-talkie.

"Loud and clear," the Chief said.

"Here we go," Agent Tompkins said with a loud sigh.

"Nice to talk to you, too, Agent Tompkins," I snapped.

"Don't start," the Chief said. "What have you got, Suzy?"

"I think you should all tie up at the docks near you," I said. "Betty and Joshua are already at the boathouse on our side waiting for Walter to land. Once you get out of your boats, you'll see paths that lead directly up the hill to the main house. You'll be able to sneak up from behind."

"Definitely," my mother said. "That's the way to go."

"Okay, sounds like a plan," the Chief said. "But stay put right where you are and out of sight."

"Will do, Chief," Rooster said, setting the radio on the seat next to him.

We watched as Coke Bottle slowed the pontoon boat and expertly maneuvered it into one of the boathouse slips. He climbed out to tie the boat off then began helping the people onboard onto the dock. Soon, a long line of people had formed. Everyone on the dock glanced around their surroundings, obviously confused. Several were bouncing up and down and hugging themselves for warmth.

"What's going on?" Agent Tompkins said over the radio.

"They're standing on the dock," Rooster said. "Are you all onshore?"

"I am," Agent Tompkins said. "Jackson is staying with the boat."

"Affirmative," one of the Coast Guard guys said. "We just landed."

"I'm halfway up the path," the Chief whispered.

"Well, it looks like they're all heading up to the house," Rooster said. "You guys might want to take cover when they get close."

"They're probably going to give them a break and let them warm up before the next leg of the trip," Agent Tompkins said.

"Maybe their plan is to spend the night here and head out in the morning," Chief Abrams said.

"Or, if their bladders are anything like mine, they need to pee," Josie said, squirming in her seat. "I'm busting."

"Let them get everyone in the house," Agent Tompkins said. "I don't want anybody to get shot."

"That would be quite a welcome to their new country," I said.

"But a great heads-up about our gun culture, huh?" Josie said.

"Chief," Agent Tompkins said. "Can you cover the back of the house?"

"No problem. It's right in front of me."

"You guys from the Coast Guard should split up and cover the sides. As soon as I get there, I'll handle the front. Once we're in place, we'll try to draw Betty and her partners outside."

"They're actually standing on the front porch," I said. "Why don't we just listen in for a few minutes? Maybe they'll make your job easier."

"Okay," Agent Tompkins said. "I like it. But keep your walkie-talkie on so we can listen in."

"You gotta love technology," I said, motioning for Rooster to hold the walkie-talkie close to a pair of headphones that worked with the microphone.

"Did you have any problems?" Betty said.

"No. We got lucky when the wind dropped," Coke Bottle said.

"Can you guys hear them?" Rooster said.

"We can," Agent Tompkins said.

Rooster pulled the anchor out of the water and set it down on the deck. The boat began to slowly drift toward the boathouse.

"Just in case they start shooting and we need to get out of here in a hurry," he said to my mother.

"Good call," Josie said. "What are they talking about?"

"They're arguing about something."

"Who is?" my mother said. "My goggles are fogged up."

"Betty and Joshua," I said, waving her off. "Shush."

"What do you think you're doing?" Joshua said, a touch of panic in his voice.

"I'm pointing a gun at you," Betty said. "What does it look like?"

"What the hell is the matter with you?" Joshua said.

"It's been fun, Josh. But I'm afraid it's over," Betty said in a voice that made the hairs on the back of my neck stand up.

"But you need me."

"To do what?" Betty said.

"To drive the boat," Joshua said. "Then we're going to the Caribbean, remember?"

"Slight change of plans," Betty said. "And I've got the idiot to drive the boat."

"Hey, who are you calling an idiot?" Coke Bottle said.

"Betty, put that thing away," Joshua said.

"In a minute," she said.

Then we heard the unmistakable *pop* of a gunshot through a silencer and Joshua dropped like a rock on the porch.

"Talk about a Black Widow," my mother said, shaking her head. "That woman is ruthless."

"There goes Coke Bottle," I said, watching as Rooster's cousin dashed across the porch and dove off the balcony.

We heard two more pops then Betty walked to the end of the porch and scanned the ground below. Cursing, she headed back to the front door and grabbed a large duffel bag off the deck before heading down the steps.

"She's taking off," Rooster said into the walkie-talkie.

"Which direction?" Agent Tompkins said.

"She's coming right at us," Rooster said, reaching for his tranquilizer gun. "It looks like the money is in a duffel bag. She's driving herself out."

"I'll get down there as soon as I can," Agent Tompkins said. "Are you still around back, Chief?"

"I am."

"Head inside the house and make sure none of the folks try to escape," Agent Tompkins said.

"They're on an island, Agent Tompkins."

"Oh, right. Just keep an eye out for Walter."

"We got him," one of the Coast Guard men said. "He was wandering around in a daze waving his hands in front of his face."

"He must have lost his glasses when he went off the porch," Rooster said, raising the tranquilizer gun.

"What are you doing?" my mother said.

"I'm going to shoot her," Rooster said. "That FBI agent isn't going to get here in time."

"Suzy, get down behind the bulkhead," my mother said in her best *I don't want to hear a word from you* voice. "You too, Josie."

We did as we were told, and I watched the action through my goggles. The boat had continued to drift toward the boathouse, and I could see the look of determination on Betty's face as she neared the dock.

"How accurate is that thing?" my mother said.

"I'm good from a hundred feet in," Rooster said. "We're close enough."

Betty reached the dock, and her trot slowed to a brisk walk as she started to make her way to the boathouse.

"Ow," Rooster said, lowering the gun as he grimaced. "Damn. That hurts."

"Another spasm?" my mother said.

"Yeah," he said, almost toppling over.

"Give me that thing," my mother said, snatching the tranquilizer gun from him and taking aim.

"Hold up a sec, Mrs. C.," Josie snapped. "Rooster, what color dart did you load?"

"Why do you care?" I said.

"Because I don't want to be charged with accessory to murder," she said. "A full dose of that sedative could kill her."

"Good to know," I said, nodding.

"It's okay," Rooster said, still holding his lower back. "It's the dose for a cub."

My mother took aim through the scope then fired. The dart hit Betty in the upper thigh, and she dropped to one knee in pain. She struggled to her feet and took a couple more steps before falling to both knees. Then she toppled forward, face first on the dock.

"What's going on?" Josie said, staring into the darkness.

"My mom shot Betty."

"I'm so glad you decided to tag along, Mrs. C."

Betty, unable to stand, began a slow crawl down the dock, dragging the duffel bag behind her, then gave it up when Agent Tompkins arrived and placed a foot firmly on her back. He bent down to grab the gun from her hand, then knelt and handcuffed her behind the back. He examined the dart protruding from her jeans then flashed two thumbs up in our direction.

"But how?" Betty eventually managed to get out.

"Suzy," Agent Tompkins said, shrugging. "I'll tell you all about it after your nap."

Rooster started the engine and moments later the boat was secured to the dock. I started to climb out but stopped when my mother grabbed my arm.

"Hang on," she said, looking at Agent Tompkins. "Make the call first."

"Got it," he said, grabbing the walkie-talkie from his belt. "What's the status, Chief?"

"We're clear," he said. "Walter is right here handcuffed to the porch railing. And all the people are safe and sound inside the house. A little confused, but definitely safe and sound."

"Okay, darling. You can go."

"If you've got questions for her, make it quick," Josie said. "She's going to be nodding off soon."

I removed the night vision goggles and rubbed the spot on my forehead where they'd been pressing hard against the skin. I grabbed Agent Tompkins' extended hand and made my way

279

onto the dock. I headed straight for Betty. She looked up at me with a dazed expression.

"You ruined everything," Betty said.

"Yeah, sorry about that."

"Did you shoot me?"

"No, my mom did. I gotta know, Betty. Why did you shoot Roger Smith?"

"He got greedy," she whispered into the dock.

"And Joshua?"

"I got greedy," she said, then giggled. "I'm going to take a little nap now."

I watched her drift off, realizing whatever other questions I had for her, and there were many, would have to wait.

"Chief," Agent Tompkins said into his walkie-talkie. "Can you find a light switch for down here?"

"Hang on," my mother said, climbing out of the boat and heading for the boathouse.

Moments later, we were bathed in light. Agent Tompkins helped Josie out of the boat.

"Would you mind carrying this up to the house?" he said, handing the duffel bag to Josie. "I'll be up in a few minutes. I need to make a couple calls."

"It's not as heavy as I would have thought," Josie said, hefting the bag.

"Two million in hundreds weighs about fifty pounds," he said.

"I did not know that," she said, heading for the path.

"Congratulations, Agent Tompkins," I said, extending my hand.

"Thanks. You too," he said as he returned the handshake. "Truce?"

"Yeah," I said with a grin. "We can at least give it a shot, huh?"

Chapter 28

Josie raced ahead of us in search of a bathroom as we headed up the path to the house.

"Hell of a shot, Mom," I said, draping an arm over her shoulder.

"Rooster taught me well," she said. "Remember that the next time you decide to get snarky with me." She looked over at Rooster. "How's your back?"

"It's fine," he said. "I just need a long, hot soak."

We climbed the front steps and came to a stop next to the Chief. Rooster glared at his cousin who refused to make eye contact.

"What happened?" the Chief said.

"My mom shot Betty with Rooster's tranquilizer gun," I said.

"Just when I thought the night couldn't get any weirder," he said.

"Where's Joshua's body?"

"I asked the Coast Guard guys to move him around back. The people inside are freaked out enough without having to deal with a dead body."

"Freddie's not going to be happy you moved the body," I said.

"Tough noogies," he said. "What are you doing, Rooster?"

"Saying hello to my cousin."

"Rooster. Don't."

"How about just one for old-time sake?"

The Chief glanced around then nodded.

"Okay. But just one."

Rooster moved in close to Coke Bottle.

"Look at me, Walter."

Coke Bottle eventually complied.

"You're going away for a long time, Walter. And I want to give you something to remember me by."

"You don't need to do that, Rooster," Coke Bottle whispered, his eyes darting back and forth.

Rooster stood directly in front of his cousin for a long time before he nodded.

"You're right, Walter," Rooster said. "If the beating I gave you the other night didn't do the trick, nothing will. I just hope you look good in orange."

"I didn't the last time," Coke Bottle said. "By the way, have you seen the dog? I've been worried about him."

"Really?" I said, staring at him.

"Yeah, I've grown fond of him. I brought him back to the island, but he was gone the next morning. I thought he might have fallen in the water."

"No, he's safe and sound. His owner is picking him up on Friday," I said.

"Good," Coke Bottle said.

"You guys want to take a look at the folks inside?" the Chief said.

I paused at the door to pick up a small backpack Betty had left behind. We followed him into the house where a couple dozen people were doing their best to relax. The majority of them were middle-aged, and various languages were being spoken. Someone had figured out how to work the remote and several people were watching soccer.

"I knew it," my mother said with a scowl as she stared at a couch. "Look at that."

I studied the large orange stain on one of the cushions and frowned at her.

"What is it?"

"Cheetos," she said. "And it looks he's been wiping his hands on the couch." She looked at Rooster. "You should have hit him when you had the chance."

A dark-haired woman with a young girl hugging one of her legs approached. She looked around tentatively, and the girl hid behind her mother and peeked out at us.

"Aren't you a cutie pie?" I said softly to the girl as I knelt down. "What's your name?"

"Gertie," the little girl whispered.

"What a pretty name. How old are you?"

"Four," she said with a wide-eyed stare that melted my heart.

"What a great age to be," I said, then stood up and extended my hand to the woman. "I'm Suzy. This is my mother, Maxine. That's Rooster. And next to him is Chief Abrams."

"It's nice to meet you. My name is Anna," the woman said, obviously nervous. "Chief? Police?"

"Yes, I'm the chief of police for a town near here."

"A lot of the others don't speak English," Anna said. "And they asked me if I could find out what's going to happen to us."

"I imagine you're all going to be sent back to your home countries," the Chief said softly. "I'm very sorry."

"Oh, no," Anna said, her lips quivering as she blinked back tears. The little girl grabbed her mother's leg with both arms and began to cry. "It's okay, Gertie. We'll figure something out."

"What's going on?" Josie said, returning from the bathroom.

"This is Anna and her daughter, Gertie," I said.

"It's nice to meet you," Josie said to the mother, then sat down on the floor. "What's the matter, Gertie?"

"The bad men are going to get us," she said, tears streaming down her face.

"Do you know what she's talking about?" Josie said, glancing up at us.

"Not yet," I said, then focused on Anna.

"Things are very dangerous for us in my country at the moment," Anna said. "My father was a political activist who chose the wrong side. Our whole family was targeted by the

285

death squads and Gertie and I are the only two who survived. My husband…" she trailed off as she glanced down at her daughter. She blinked back tears as she shook her head. "Gertie and I barely made it out of the country. And if we're forced to go back, well…"

"Yeah, I got it," I whispered.

"Are there others here who are in the same predicament?" my mother said.

"No, I don't think so," Anna said. "Most of them are just looking for a better way of life and have the money to pay for it."

"I see," my mother said, glancing at the Chief. Then she looked back at Anna. "What sort of work did you do in your home country?"

"I'm a doctor," she said. "What you would call a general practitioner. But I've done a lot of work with children. Many of them were wounded in the fighting."

"A doctor? You don't say," my mother said, again catching the Chief's eye.

"No way," the Chief whispered, slowly shaking his head.

"Why not?" my mother said.

The penny dropped for me, and I gave my mother's hand an affectionate squeeze.

"That's asking a lot, Maxine," the Chief said.

"Who's ever gonna know?" she said softly.

"I'm sorry," Anna said, watching the scene play out. "But I'm not following."

"Don't worry, you will," my mother said, smiling at her. Then she stared at the Chief.

The Chief eventually shrugged then walked to the door and took a look down at the dock where Agent Tompkins was still talking on the phone. He returned and nodded at the backpack I was holding.

"Are the fake IDs in there?" he said.

"They are," I said, scanning the contents.

"Find their papers," he said. "But don't make a production out of it."

I flipped through the bundles of documents and found the two in question. But I kept my hand in the backpack.

"You paid two hundred thousand for you and your daughter, right?" the Chief said.

"Yes, it was everything we had," Anna said.

The Chief nodded at Josie who reached into the duffel bag and slipped several bundles of cash under her coat.

"Okay," the Chief said, glancing around the room to make sure we weren't being watched. "Maxine, you're going to take Anna and Gertie someplace where they won't be seen for the next hour or so."

"The downstairs suite," my mother said.

"Perfect," I said, removing the documents from the backpack and sliding them inside my coat. I smiled at Anna then bent down in front of the little girl. "How would you like to see the rest of the house, Gertie?"

"Okay," she said softly.

"I'll join you in a minute, Mom."

"Please, follow me," my mother said, slowly leading them toward the back of the house.

I gave Chief Abrams the biggest hug I could muster then let go but continued to grasp his shoulders.

"You've done something truly magnificent, Chief," I said, staring directly into his eyes as I felt mine begin to water.

"I couldn't live with myself knowing I sent them back," he whispered. He wiped his eyes with both hands then exhaled loudly. "And your mom's right. Who's ever gonna know?"

"As long as the documents and money match the number of people they take out of here, nobody," Josie said.

"What a day," Rooster said, rubbing his lower back.

"How many laws do you think we've broken tonight?" the Chief said.

"Don't worry about it, Chief," Josie said with a shrug. "What are you going to do? Call the cops?"

Epilogue

Due to the previous day's storm, attendance was light at our eleven o'clock seating. Which was a good thing because of the influx of twenty-two guests who'd been invited at the last moment. The other two, a young mother and her gorgeous daughter, were at my mom's house about to experience their first Thanksgiving dinner.

"Okay, I'll be back soon," my mother said, carrying the two bags of food Chef Claire had assembled. "Save me some turkey." She headed out the back door of the restaurant.

"Can we give you a hand?" I said to Chef Claire.

"No, I think we're good in here," she said. "But if you could help out in the dining room, that would be great."

"You got it," I said, gesturing for Josie to follow me.

We entered the dining room and looked around. I spotted Agent Tompkins at a table with Jackson and Rooster.

"Good morning," Agent Tompkins said, sliding two chairs back from the table. "Happy Thanksgiving."

"You're in a good mood," I said. "Hey, Jackson."

"Hi, guys. Happy Thanksgiving," Jackson said. "It sounds like I missed all the action last night while I was keeping an eye on the boat."

"Yeah, it was…eventful," I said.

"One for the ages," Josie said. "I know I'll never forget it."

"How's your back, Rooster?"

"Much better, thanks," he said, then stared down at his plate. "So many choices. Where do I begin?"

"Work the outside edges first," Josie said. "It cuts down on the spillage factor."

"What did your bosses in Washington have to say?" I said.

"Well, they're obviously delighted we were able to bust up the trafficking ring," he said. "But they were blown away by the news about Betty."

"Where is she?"

"She and Walter are in a van heading for the FBI office in Buffalo," he said. "A couple days of questioning, then she'll be charged with a very long list of crimes."

"What did she have to say about her relationship with Joshua?"

"Not much," he said, slicing off a piece of turkey. "She's already lawyered up." He chewed, savored, then swallowed. "But it doesn't matter. She'll talk eventually."

"Have you guys been able to get a look at her financials?" I said.

"We have," he said, attacking a pile of stuffing. "She had almost nine million. Not counting the two million and change we recovered last night."

"She was so close to pulling it off."

"She was indeed," he said, then swallowed and took a sip of water. "Hey, what was the number of people we thought were being brought in last night?"

I glanced at Josie then stared off for a moment.

"I think it was twenty-two," I said. "How many were there last night?"

"Twenty-two," he said, dredging a piece of turkey through gravy. "But I could have sworn we were talking about two dozen."

"Somebody was probably just rounding off," I said.

"Yeah, I'm sure you're right," he said. "And all the documents and money tied out perfectly, so, case closed."

"Well done," I said, pushing my chair back from the table. "We need to run. We've got tables to clear and dessert to serve."

"I understand," Agent Tompkins said. "Thanks again, Suzy."

"Are you sticking around for a few days?" Josie said. "Chef Claire would love that."

"Believe me, I tried to make it happen," he said. "But I have to go to Buffalo to lead the questioning."

"Maybe next time," I said. "Come on up when you get a chance to take a vacation."

"Or I could invite Chef Claire to D.C."

"It's worth a shot," Josie said, waving goodbye as we left the table.

"That worked out well," I said.

"Score one for the good guys," she said.

"We should do something extra special for the Chief at Christmas."

"Like a free check-up?"

"Funny. You want to eat now or wait?"

"Let's wait," she said. "We should be able find time between the eleven and two o'clock sittings."

"Works for me," I said, then spotted my mother entering the dining room from the kitchen closely followed by Chef Claire. "How are they doing?"

"Wonderful," she said, glancing around the room. "They're currently devouring their dinner. I think it's been a few days since they've eaten."

"I'll never forget the look on little Gertie's face when she was hanging on for dear life to her mom's leg," Josie said. "A four-year-old shouldn't have to deal with fear like that."

"You got that right," I whispered, nodding as I subconsciously rubbed my stomach. I turned to my mom. "So, what's the plan?"

"On Monday, I'll take Anna to meet the town council. Then I'll introduce her to everyone at the hospital."

"What are you going to tell them about where you found her?" I said.

"I'll come up with something," she said with a grin. "Would you mind babysitting Gertie on Monday?"

292

"We'd love to," I said. "She can spend the day with the dogs."

"Thank you, darling. Josie, am I correct your house down the street from the Inn is vacant at the moment?"

"It is. They're more than welcome to move in."

"Perfect," my mother said. "I love it when things work out."

"Especially things that don't have a chance to work out if you say no to opportunities," I said.

"Don't gloat, darling. It's not becoming," she said, taking another look around. "It looks like our European guests are enjoying their meals."

"It's the least we could do," I said. "What's going to happen to them?"

"Chief Abrams said they'll be bussed to New York then put on planes back to where they came from," she said. "It's sad when you think about it. But at least they're going to get their money back."

"And they'll be able to say they had a traditional Thanksgiving dinner," Josie said.

"Probably small consolation," I said.

"And rather ironic," Chef Claire said. "Since they're probably not feeling very thankful today."

"Indeed," my mother said. "Okay, let's take advantage of the temporary lull and take the photo."

"Let me go grab, Charlie," Chef Claire said, ducking her head into the kitchen.

293

We took our usual spot in front of the fireplace with me next to my mother and Josie and Chef Claire on either side. Charlie motioned us closer together then fiddled with the camera.

"Our third year," I said. "And next year they'll be five of us."

"There's already five of us, darling."

"You're right, Mom."

My mother gently placed a hand on my protruding belly. Josie and Chef Claire followed suit. Then I placed a hand on top and pressed tight, hopefully sending a message to my daughter she had nothing to worry about it.

About what her life would be like.

Or if she would be safe.

More importantly, we were sending her a message that she was loved, and would be loved well.

For forever and a day.